"All right." He came up beside her and covered one of her chilled hands with his.

"What if we enjoy what is sure to be an outstanding dinner and then head back to my place and handle whatever is coming together as husband and wife?"

She studied his profile, seeing none of the tension or stress in the hard square of his jaw, only resolute determination. "Together?" She was bewildered as much by the offer as she was by the easy way he delivered it.

"Exactly." He faced her, giving her a heated, toe-curling smile.

If only it would be that easy. "You stepping up publicly as my husband could very well put Gray Box at risk."

"I've factored that in."

His absolute fearlessness despite the unknowns made her want him more. She hadn't known it was possible to sink deeper into her infatuation with him.

"You expect me to live with you at your condo?"

MARRIAGE CONFIDENTIAL

USA TODAY Bestselling Authors

DEBRA WEBB &
REGAN BLACK

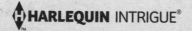
HARLEQUIN INTRIGUE®

For my grandmother, ever the diplomat in the family,
for being a boundless source of wisdom, inspiration
and unconditional love.

—Regan

ISBN-13: 978-0-373-75686-5

Recycling programs
for this product may
not exist in your area.

Marriage Confidential

Copyright © 2017 by Debra Webb

Printed in U.S.A.

www.Harlequin.com

Debra Webb, born in Alabama, wrote her first story at age nine and her first romance at thirteen. It wasn't until after she spent three years working for the military behind the Iron Curtain—and a five-year stint with NASA—that she realized her true calling. Since then the *USA TODAY* bestselling author has penned more than one hundred novels, including her internationally bestselling Colby Agency series.

Regan Black, a *USA TODAY* bestselling author, writes award-winning, action-packed novels featuring kick-butt heroines and the sexy heroes who fall in love with them. Raised in the Midwest and California, she and her family, along with their adopted greyhound, two arrogant cats and a quirky finch, reside in the South Carolina Lowcountry, where the rich blend of legend, romance and history fuels her imagination.

Books by Debra Webb and Regan Black

Harlequin Intrigue

Investigating Christmas
Marriage Confidential

Colby Agency: Family Secrets

Gunning for the Groom
Heavy Artillery Husband

The Specialists: Heroes Next Door

The Hunk Next Door
Heart of a Hero
To Honor and To Protect
Her Undercover Defender

Visit the Author Profile page at Harlequin.com for more titles.

CAST OF CHARACTERS

Sam Bellemere—A cutting edge software developer, technology genius and billionaire, he serves as head of security for Gray Box, a company he founded with his old friend Rush Grayson.

Madison Goode—A State Department liaison working in San Francisco, California, she is part of a team that maintains peaceful, open communication between the United States, China and Vietnam.

Xi Liu—The highest ranking official on station at the Chinese consulate in San Francisco. He has been working closely with Madison on a new exhibit of treasures from China, on view at a museum in San Francisco.

Rush Grayson—Rush pulled himself out of a bleak childhood and a stint in juvenile detention with Sam for hacking secure websites to create Gray Box, considered the best option for storing data in the information security industry. Newly married to Lucy Gaines.

Lucy Gaines Grayson—A new addition to the Gray Box team, Lucy brings a fresh viewpoint and energy the executive staff appreciates. Newly married to Rush Grayson.

Chapter One

Shoulders back, head high, Madison Goode kept pace with the silent and stoic Special Agent Spalding from the FBI at her side. Her high heels clicked softly on the exquisite black marble tile. The sound was the only acknowledgment of their progress. Every inch of the Artistry of the Far East Museum was elegantly appointed and thoughtfully designed, not just the galleries displaying the invaluable collection. To Madison, who'd been behind the scenes of many of the most elaborate venues here and around the world, it seemed as if the museum founders had been as eager to inspire the staff as they were the visitors. She appreciated such excellent attention to detail.

As she turned her wrist to check her watch, her platinum and diamond wedding set glowed beautifully under the perfect lighting. She'd had it cleaned yesterday for this occasion, a little unnerved by how awkward and vulnerable she felt in the hours it wasn't on her finger. She took comfort in the familiarity of the jewelry in its rightful place, a calming reminder in what hopefully wouldn't blow up into a crisis.

The countdown for the evening was running in her head. The dignitaries from China's foreign ministry would be here within forty-five minutes for a pregala toast and a private viewing of the new exhibit on loan to the United States. She knew from her years of experience as a State Department liaison that they would arrive five minutes earlier than scheduled.

Special Agent Spalding held open the door, encouraging her to enter the museum security office ahead of him. Even here, in the controlled lighting, she noted the aesthetic details that would empower the staff and boost efficiency. Her gaze slid over the monitors and the personnel watching each screen and status panel. No one was panicking and everything seemed to be in order, yet the tension simmering in the air was completely different than on her previous visits during the negotiation of the exhibit. When Spalding requested— demanded—her review of a potential security breach, he'd explained the threat was not as clear and easy to locate as a thief lurking in the building for his chance to strike.

"Technicians monitoring the computer systems found a problem," Spalding said, his voice startling her after the long minutes of silence.

She followed him over to a small work space at the far end of the room. Although Madison had met with the cyber security managers on her previous visits, she'd only been introduced to the full team once. She smiled at the man and woman—very early twenties at best— wearing museum security uniform shirts with skinny jeans. Clearly uncertain how to proceed, they stood nervously beside their workstations where two FBI agents in subdued suits had assumed their seats and were working feverishly on their computers.

Madison's stomach twisted, but years of practice and discipline had perfected her ability to hide any outward signs of distress or insecurity. She extended her hand to the woman first and introduced herself. "Madison Goode, State Department. Special Agent Spalding tells me you've found some kind of threat?"

"Yes. I'm Carli," the woman said as she bobbed her head. Her bright red glasses framed blue eyes highlighted by purple mascara. Her pursed lips and scowl gave away her exasperation at being pushed from her station. "We were handling it."

"Devon," the man beside her said. He unfolded his arms long enough to shake Madison's proffered hand and bump up his round, wire-framed glasses. Arms crossed once more, the fingers of one hand drummed against his opposite arm. She recognized how eager he was to get his hands back on his keyboard. "Carli and I saw the chatter about the attack and followed protocol," he explained.

"These two just took over," Carli said.

"We could be helping," the two finished in unison.

Special Agent Spalding cleared his throat and gave a small tilt of his head. At the signal, Madison motioned for the technicians to step aside with her. "You did exactly the right thing," she assured them. "Thank you both.

I'm sure the FBI will only require another few minutes to make an assessment. Can you walk me through it, please?"

"We've been gearing up for weeks," Carli began. "Staff meetings, search parameters—"

"And likely troublemakers," Devon interjected. "There hadn't been a whisper of a problem until an hour ago."

"Then we found the chat room," Carli continued. "Chatter about how America was selling the country to China one piece of art at a time. We saw blatant threats to the new exhibit. A rallying cry to take a stand."

"Ugly stuff, really," Devon added. "We notified our manager, took screenshots and started tracking usernames—"

"And IP addresses," Carli finished.

By the time Madison had heard the entire story, she was nearly convinced Carli and Devon were twins with the way they completed each other's sentences. The FBI agents at the stations continued working as Devon and Carli grew increasingly impatient. "I promise they'll be out of your space as soon as possible," Madison said.

Devon snorted and Carli elbowed him with a whispered reminder to be polite. Although

Madison hadn't hit thirty yet, these two suddenly made her feel old as they fidgeted and murmured in tech-speak about the situation.

Catching Spalding's eye, she walked over. "Any progress?"

"Looks as if a group of American radicals is making a legitimate threat," Spalding replied. "What my team is unraveling implies a direct, credible threat on the delegation from China. You need to postpone the reception. Possibly delay the exhibit."

In her head, she raged and screamed, though she kept her expression neutral and her breathing under control. This unprecedented exhibit was scheduled to open to the public tomorrow. Ticket sales had exceeded their projections and officials at the Chinese consulate were openly thrilled. Delaying tonight's event would undermine significant progress in the diplomatic arena and she wasn't ready to toss that out the window, yet she couldn't put lives or the displays at risk. "Can you run the vocabulary and threats against the emails our office received earlier this month?"

"Yes." He signaled his crews to do as she asked. Spalding was grim, his voice low as he continued, "From all appearances this group is organized and ready to strike." He went on with an explanation of his on-site security team and standard precautions. FBI and local police both in uniform and undercover had the museum surrounded and the Chinese delegation's route from the consulate to the museum under surveillance, as well. "When we discussed this last week, we decided those emails came from a hacktivist group based in Asia."

"The internet brings people together," she replied. She braced a hand on the edge of the desk and leaned forward. Her sleek ponytail slid over her shoulder as she reviewed each correspondence and she pushed it back as she straightened. "The language is quite similar." Similar enough that she was almost positive they were being strung along, dancing to someone else's agenda.

Security wasn't her assigned area of expertise and yet Madison needed to weigh all threats and consequences to the exhibit and the Chinese delegation. The political fallout of canceling the event or postponing the opening could be a serious problem. Her intuition told her they had trouble, though she disagreed with Spalding that the trouble would strike in the form of an immediate personal attack.

"The radicals on the other side of that computer screen are noisemakers," she said decisively. "They've never struck in person. We're prepared and we'll continue with the program as scheduled."

Spalding's eyes were hard and his voice was barely audible. "If you're wrong?"

Since accepting her role within the State Department, she'd been walking the tenuous line of relations between China, Vietnam and other interested parties in the South China Sea long enough to trust her gut instinct. "There is trouble, I'll grant you, but it is *not* a physical threat tonight. Someone is playing us, saying enough of the right things to make us doubt and potentially cause a rift. I refuse to make a decision based on fear that will undo the progress we've made in the past year."

Spalding glared down at her and only her years of ballet training kept her spine straight, her gaze direct. "Listen, Goode, if you—"

"Sir! Ma'am!"

Madison peered around Spalding to see a member of the museum security staff waving frantically from the various readouts that confirmed priceless objets d'art and artifacts were secure in their displays. "What is it?" Spalding demanded as he crossed the room, Madison on his heels.

Her famous self-control almost snapped when she saw which exhibit caused the concern. The first troubling email her office had intercepted two weeks ago specifically mentioned the cup with dragon handles carved from white jade. The cup signified more than exceptional artistry and craftsmanship. Bringing a prized item from twelfth-century China to this museum in America indicated growing trust between their countries. Priceless, it wasn't the oldest piece China had shared in this exhibit, but certainly one of the best known. Any impression that it wasn't secure could destabilize the agreement.

"We read a spike in the display temperature first," the man at the controls explained, bringing up a graph. "Now the electronic lock is flickering."

"Flickering? What does that mean?" Spalding asked.

Madison already knew. She'd been through the museum a dozen times already, reviewing every detail of the items selected as well as the security measures necessary to protect the extraordinary exhibit China planned to share as a gesture of good intentions. A flickering electronic lock meant someone either was in the security system right now or had planted a virus to weaken it.

While Spalding sent his team along with museum staff to verify the safety of the cup and secure the galleries, she pulled her phone from her clutch and prepared to make an uncomfortable call. Whether or not the cup or any of the other priceless treasures were stolen tonight, a perceived flaw in the security would raise suspicion. She debated with herself over how to keep the head of the consular staff informed without wrecking the confidence she'd worked so hard to establish.

She turned to the man still monitoring the control panels. "Is it possible to isolate what type of interference is affecting the lock?"

"I can do that." Carli stepped up when the technician hesitated.

Madison watched the younger woman conduct a swift search of the programming until she found what they were all looking for. Madison wasn't an expert in computer languages or coding, but she recognized enough groupings on the monitor. The source of the problem in the locking mechanism on the display case was a hacker who'd been pounding at the State Department computer system firewalls in a chaotic effort to make his point about the insecurities plaguing the world. The official position was the hacker was tilting at windmills for the sheer joy of annoying cyber security. Now Madison wondered what they had overlooked. Only a thorough investigation would determine if this stunt was a timely coincidence or if he was in fact part of the outrageous, threatening chatter Carli and Devon had discovered.

"This is a hacker," Madison stated. She kept her opinions and curses to herself as she opened a menu on her cell phone and located the right name in her contact list. "The reception and gala will go on. I want security increased around the cup please," she said to Spalding. "Carli, please take a screenshot and do what you can to hold the hacker's attention," she added.

"I can help her." Devon plugged in a wireless keyboard and jumped into the technological fray. "How much do you want us to do?"

"Don't strike back directly," Madison said, keeping the phone to her ear. She listened as the line rang and rang, hoping for a miracle. From what they'd been coping with at the office in recent weeks, she suspected the hacker was better than Carli and Devon, even combined. "Make him jump through enough hoops that it keeps him entertained." Madison wrote her cell phone number on a notepad and left it between them. "Keep me in the loop."

"You got it," Carli and Devon said in unison.

As she left the security suite, Madison heard Spalding reorganizing his staff and she hit the redial icon. Again, the one man she needed didn't answer and her call went to voice mail. Irritation plucked at the tense muscles in her neck and shoulders. *She* had answered immediately when he needed her last year. Of course, he'd reached out by email that day. Rethinking her approach, she disconnected the call and opened her email application. After entering an admittedly desperate message, she hit Send. All she could do now was wait and hope Carli and Devon would be enough.

She made a last-minute adjustment to the guest list in case her secret-weapon expert did show up, alerting the team assigned to the rear entrance of the museum. Ignoring the raised eyebrows and a low whistle at the name she added, she headed for the main museum entrance. The lead dignitaries from the Chinese consulate would arrive within minutes.

"Hope you're right about this," Spalding muttered, his gaze sweeping the area.

"I am," she replied with more confidence than she felt. There would be time for recriminations and self-doubt later when she was home alone. Plenty of time if this became an assassination attempt, since she'd either be dead or unemployed by morning.

Minutes later the formal greetings were exchanged on the red carpet outside and she gave her full attention to the delegation while Spalding watched everything else. Everyone in this first, exclusive group from China appeared as relaxed as she'd ever seen them as she guided them into the museum entrance hall. The invitations had specified black-tie and she thought the group resembled a stunning kaleidoscope with the colorful silk dresses of the women spiraling about the backdrop of black tuxedos.

Madison treated herself to an inward sigh of relief when the first group was safely inside, smiling and greeting senior staff from the State Department as well as the museum director, Edward Wong. Stepping out of view, she confirmed preparations were on schedule for the champagne toast in front of the prized white jade cup.

Brief, scripted speeches were exchanged between officials along with gestures of confidence and trust. If the hacker had attempted to rattle a saber on the Chinese side, the group showed no signs of distress. For the first time in over an hour, she believed the evening would run without any visible hitch.

At either side of the doorway to the premier gallery, golden champagne sparkled and bubbled in narrow crystal flutes ready for guests. Seeing that the key players from China and America were all smiles as they gathered together around the white jade cup display, Madison wanted to give a victorious cheer. With the drama and bids for power that filled the news most days, creating these moments of peace and goodwill was the big payoff in a career she loved.

She'd met and spoken with every person scheduled to work in this room, down to the museum security guards posted discreetly at intervals throughout the gallery and museum at large. Before she could fully relax, her phone vibrated against her palm. The incoming text message had her smothering a wince, arriving too late for her to clear the room.

Suddenly the lighting flickered inside the display case of the white jade cup and the lock buzzed and clicked. With everyone so close, there was no chance for the problem to go unnoticed. The hacker had grown bored with Carli and Devon and was obviously exerting his control on the system. Across the room, Madison saw the museum director bring the guards to attention as Spalding issued orders for his team.

Xi Liu, the highest ranking official on station at the Chinese consulate, aimed straight for Madison. They had worked closely with the museum staff in preparing for this exhibit. "What is the meaning of this?" he demanded.

Mr. Wong joined her immediately. An older gentleman and first-generation American born to Chinese parents, he remained fluent in both the language and the behavioral expectations. "This is a standard test," he explained calmly to Mr. Liu. "My apologies for the incorrect timing. This is a routine we typically employ after closing. The schedule change must have reverted. I assure you all is well and your generous exhibit is secure." Mr. Wong's serene expression was tested when the lock whirred and buzzed again. "There are no weaknesses in the system that prevent us from displaying the piece publicly."

Mr. Liu didn't appear entirely convinced as he turned to Madison. "You assured me all was in place. What is happening?"

"As you are aware, sir," she began, "cutting edge technology is often finicky." Madison felt a bead of sweat slide down her back. Where was the backup she'd called in? "Despite the mistiming of the normal security routine, your exhibit is quite safe." She extended an arm to indicate the room. "The collection, in fact, the entire museum, is guarded by the finest technology systems as well as by the finest personnel. Your guests and friends remain unconcerned. In fact, they appear quite eager to continue with the festivities."

Barely appeased, Mr. Liu motioned a man forward and murmured at his ear. To Madison and the director he said, "My man will stand guard with yours."

"Absolutely," she agreed. The director nodded with her. "If you would feel more comfortable, we can adjust the access of reception attendees." It wouldn't be too difficult to keep traffic out of this room and there had been no trouble at all in any other gallery. She didn't believe for a moment that theft of the cup or any other object was on the hacker's mind. Whoever had launched this attack was interested in dealing chaos and fostering mistrust. She sensed the true goal was to create a rift that would set back relations indefinitely.

Although Mr. Liu politely declined the offer to restrict access, Madison understood the nuances in his statement that emphasized his displeasure. She escorted the dignitaries from both countries to the receiving line to greet guests and checked her phone for any new messages.

Still nothing. Carli and Devon would have to find a way to end this game. Madison struggled to stay calm on her return to the security suite. The man might be out of town. If so, she'd excuse this lack of response. However, if she found out he was simply ignoring her calls and emails, she'd find Sam Bellemere and put a hammer through his most precious hard drive.

Chapter Two

Sam Bellemere sank into the plush seat of the limousine and tugged at his bow tie, letting the ends hang loose. He popped the button at the collar of his tuxedo shirt and pushed his hands through his hair. Able to breathe at last, he felt a thousand times better than he had just ten minutes ago surrounded by a ballroom full of wealthy people eager to support the Gray Box youth programs. The June fund-raiser was the one event his business partner, Rush Grayson, refused to let him dodge. The codevelopers' proprietary encryption technology had led to their founding of the cloud storage service giant, Gray Box. For the former smart-ass teenage hackers, mentoring the next generation of responsible computer geeks was a cause near and dear to both of them.

Knowing how shy Sam was, Rush had willingly assumed the role as the front man of the company, handling most of the public events and meetings. It had become an ideal partnership over the years. Rush's extroverted nature thrived on time spent in the limelight and Sam happily kept himself behind the scenes. Without Rush and the company, Sam knew he'd be labeled an eccentric hermit—or worse—by now. The label held a certain appeal for Sam, but his friend insisted that kind of notoriety set a bad example for the kids they were trying to help.

"Back to the office, sir?" asked Jake, one of the drivers Gray Box kept on staff.

"Please," Sam replied. The privacy screen rolled up between them and he withdrew his phone from the inner pocket of his jacket and turned it on. Within a minute, the device buzzed and chimed as if he'd been offline for weeks rather than hours.

He shook his head, skimming the alerts he'd missed while rubbing elbows with San Francisco's elite. No phone was another rule for social events that Sam wasn't allowed to argue with. He and Rush both knew if he'd had his phone on, he would have hidden behind the device rather than mingle face-to-face with the guests. Per their agreement, that behavior would have meant Sam was required to attend another event later in the year to make up for the gaffe.

Once a year in the monkey suit, smiling until his face ached, was more than enough time in the spotlight for Sam. Didn't matter that by the sole measure of net worth he was technically one of the elite he struggled to connect with.

Terminally shy, he felt like a fish out of water in social situations. Anything more than dinner out with his closest friends left him wound tighter than a high wire. After several awkward failures, he'd met with counselors and psychiatrists to help him, without much success. He tried chemistry as well, in the form of medication to erase his anxiety. The unpleasant side effects hadn't been worth it. He'd since resigned himself to limiting his social exposure and created a recovery plan that involved a double shot of whiskey and an online warfare game as a reward for making the attempt.

Several missed calls were from the same number, one he didn't recognize. Half a dozen emails with a similar time stamp caught his full attention. With luck, this would be a security crisis at Gray Box that only he could resolve. Then Rush would have to let him keep his phone on during future events.

To Sam's astonishment, all of the messages were from Madison Goode, an old friend from high school. Well, he'd known her for the two years he was allowed to attend public high school after his stint in juvenile detention. The government hadn't appreciated the skill or restraint when Sam and Rush hacked into sites just to prove it could be done.

Sam had tutored Madison through a couple of classes, helping her pump up her GPA as well as her comprehension on some required course work. To this day, she sent him an email Christmas card every year. As much as he resisted those conventional traditions, because she respected his preference for digital correspondence, he always sent one back.

He put the voice mail on speaker and listened, then quickly read and reread the emails, each more desperate than the last, which was only two sentences: "Come on, Sam. You owe me."

Sam shifted to the seat closer to the driver and lowered the privacy screen. "Change of plans. I need to get to the Artistry of the Far East Museum." He buttoned up his collar and started on his tie. "Fast as you can get there."

He hit Reply on the last email, letting Madison know he was on the way. Her first email had arrived over two and a half hours ago. Damn. He never would've left her hanging intentionally. She was right, he did owe her. Big time. Just before Christmas, she'd helped bring Rush and Lucy, Rush's new wife, home from France, sparing everyone involved delays and inquiries that were better off as unconfirmed rumors. Next, he tapped the icon and returned one of her three phone calls. She didn't pick up. He left a voice mail message that he was on the way.

While the driver made quick work of the bottlenecks of Friday night traffic, Sam checked for any breaking news at the museum. He came up empty and was ready to start a different search when the driver hit a detour about a block from the museum. "Looks like some big event," Jake said. "There's a red carpet out and everything."

A red carpet event with no news teams nearby? It didn't make sense. "No problem.

I'll walk from here." His curiosity piqued, Sam reached for the door handle.

"Do you want me to wait?"

"Not necessary. I can call if I need something."

Before he'd exited the limo, the familiar tension lanced across his shoulders and turned his mouth dry. At least at this event, without Rush nearby to glare at him, he could use his phone as a shield if necessary. Although he was dressed for it, he didn't want to brave the red carpet, so he turned away at the last second and looked for a side entrance. The museum was crawling with local uniforms as well as a team that gave Sam the impression the President of the United States might be in attendance. He hoped not. Rush's last meeting at the Pentagon had become urban legend in certain circles by now.

Sam took comfort again in the lack of news crews. For a split second, he considered the fallout if he walked away and caught a cab home. He waged an internal argument that there wasn't any kind of favor worth the agony of walking into a world of strangers.

But he couldn't do that. Madison had used her connections for him, coming through in the midst of a crisis to smooth over what might easily have been an unpleasant international incident for Rush, Lucy and the company. Not to mention she was one of two people from high school—aside from teachers—who consistently kept up with him. The other was Rush.

He was climbing the stairs to the side entrance, still waging that internal debate, when a uniformed museum guard and a man in a dark suit holding a tablet blocked the door. "Sam Bellemere," he told the man in the suit. As the man brought the guest list onto the tablet, Sam saw names and photos in two columns. "Madison Goode asked me to stop by," he added, shamelessly dropping her name to speed things up. "Is she here?"

The suit didn't reply, focused on scrolling through the long list. From Sam's view, he could see the last page was a different color and to his surprise, he recognized the head shot used on all of the Gray Box publicity.

"Mr. Bellemere." The suit said the name with reverence and a little shock. As he stuck out his hand, a smile erased the stoic gatekeeper's expression. "It is a *pleasure* to meet you." He pumped Sam's hand and then signaled for the museum guard to open the door. "I'll walk you back."

"Thank you."

"It is a pleasure," the suit repeated. "I'm Brady Cortland. Has Madison mentioned me? I've been on her planning team for this exhibition and reception from the start."

"Not that I recall," Sam said. Why did this guy think Madison shared any details about her work? When the man's face fell, he knew he had to say something. "But I'm terrible with names."

"No problem," Brady said. "Everyone who knows anything has heard how your work consumes you. Give me Mandarin any day over a computer language."

"You and Madison must have worked night and day on this event," Sam guessed.

"Yes!" Brady's smile reappeared. "It took most of the office at one point or another. This exhibit was a logistical nightmare," he said conspiratorially, "but so worth it in the long run." He paused outside a door marked Security. "I need to get back to my post. Madison will be relieved you're here. If you can sort out this mess, you'll be the most popular spouse in the State Department."

Sam was sure he'd misheard the man, but when he stepped inside the room, the question faded to the back of his mind. Here, surrounded by technology and the low murmurs of voices, he was instantly at home. Monitors showed views of the museum inside and out. Panels of status displays offered rows and blocks of colors and the soft click and clack of keyboards in action created his favorite background music. This tech-filled room was a world he understood.

Madison's gaze collided with his immediately. As she crossed the room, her face was the epitome of calm with not a single sign of the tension he'd heard on his voice mail and in the unhappy tenor of her emails. She was a vision in a black sleeveless dress that poured over her curves, slits high at each leg allowing her to move with the dancer's grace he remembered from school.

"You came," she said. Her lips, painted a deep red, curved into a warm smile. Her soft green eyes, framed with long black eyelashes, drifted over him head to toe and back up again. She'd pulled her blond hair back from her face. "Dressed for the occasion too." She leaned back and studied him and he wondered what she saw.

"I would've been here earlier if my phone hadn't been turned off." Her eyebrows arched. "Rush's orders for social events," he explained.

He soaked up every detail of her. They hadn't seen each other in person since their ten-year high-school reunion, another event Rush had forced him to attend. Madison had been the only bright light that evening. He remembered her in a softer dress, her hair in loose waves around her shoulders. Tonight, the sleek dress and hair created the illusion of a blond version of perfect Far Eastern elegance. As if being shy wasn't bad enough, her lithe dancer's body left him tongue-tied. He knew it would be polite to offer her a compliment. If only he could trust his mouth to deliver the words in the proper, flattering order. The years of exercises in composure and confidence in social settings were lost in the ether of his brain. He was terrified of saying something wrong in front of so many people. These were her coworkers and he wouldn't compound her current trouble with some embarrassing blunder.

Apparently understanding his discomfiture,

she leaned close and feathered a kiss near his cheek. "Thank you for coming." When she took his hand, her tight grasp was his only clue to her distress. "Did we pull you away from something important?"

"No. I'd finished my part for the evening."

Her hand slid over his arm as she guided him to a workstation. "My apologies for being simultaneously vague and persistent," she began in that perfect, unaccented voice. "I wasn't comfortable putting the details in an email. As this evening approached, we had the typical threats against the dignitaries from China and the exhibit that opens tonight with this gala reception. I chalked it up to normal background noise until the museum system was breached a few hours ago. Whoever is behind this has disrupted display settings and the electronic locks on the centerpiece of this exhibit. The consensus is if those settings can be reset, he can do more damage at will to any part of the museum."

"Sounds about right," Sam said. "Is the primary concern preventing a theft?"

"On that we all disagree. I find the threat of a theft low." She gave a quick shake of her head. "I can't rule it out, of course. The head of the Chinese consulate has added his men to the security team. If theft is the goal, a hacker messing with the display through the computer has made their task additionally difficult. I'm more concerned with what's going on in here." She circled her finger at the nearest monitor.

Her voice rolled over him as easily as surf kissing sand before it slid back to the ocean. He could listen to her for hours, a strange revelation for a man who preferred working either in near-silence or to the pounding beat of heavy metal music. Bending forward, he reached up to bump his glasses and hit his nose, forgetting he'd worn contacts. Hoping she hadn't noticed, he examined several screenshots of coding. "You caught this?" he asked, impressed.

She laughed. "No." She rolled her hand, inviting two younger people into the conversation. "Carli and Devon noticed some increasing negative chatter directly tied to the event this evening. The primary person in the chat room had too many specifics of the agenda tonight for it to be random. The FBI has been running down the source, which left Carli and Devon to try and amuse the hacker until you could get here. Pardon me," she said. "Carli and Devon, this is Sam Bellemere."

"O-M-G." Carli clapped a hand over her mouth. Her blue eyes were huge behind her glasses. "I cannot believe you married Sam Bellemere. You're the—"

"Mastermind of Gray Box," Devon said, finishing her sentence. "We're *huge* fans," he gushed.

They both tried to shake his hand simultaneously and Sam laughed it off. Though he'd never be completely comfortable in the spotlight, their overwhelming greeting gave him a pleasant distraction from another mention of marriage. Marrying Madison—or any woman—wasn't something he considered forgettable.

Reflexively he looked at her hand and caught the wedding set on her left ring finger. It was timeless and elegant, much like the woman wearing it. The classic beauty of the wedding set contrasted with the larger ruby ring on her right hand that accented the sleek lines of her dress. So he hadn't misheard the suit with the tablet. Madison had listed him as her *husband*?

"Was Rush your best man?" Carli asked.

"If we could stay on point," Madison interjected coolly.

Happily, Sam thought. Whatever her reasons for calling him her husband, he trusted she'd tell him later. He wouldn't embarrass her with questions now, in front of people who clearly respected her. "What do you need?" He reached for the mouse and scrolled through the screenshots Carli and Devon had captured.

"I need to know the white jade cup and the museum as a whole are secure and will stay secure. This exhibit is a huge honor for the US and a big show of trust from China. Any perceived trouble could undo months of negotiations." She waved over another man. "If you'd coordinate with Special Agent Spalding, I need to circulate with the guests for a few minutes."

"Sure." He pulled out a chair and sat down. Within a few keystrokes, he was into the museum system and feeling his way around. He'd much rather be here than out there with her among a crowd of strangers.

While Spalding brought him up to speed, Sam felt Carli and Devon watching every keystroke as he looked for how the hacker had wormed this code into the display controls.

The code caught his full attention and everything around him faded into the background. He was always happier working with computer code than trying to unravel the mysteries of people. People had secrets and hidden agendas such as pretend marriage. Computer code, no matter how convoluted or infectious, always retained a sense of logic, if only to the coder. He couldn't imagine how Madison managed all the protocols and people day in and day out. He'd go crazy under that kind of pressure.

As he worked, he kept up a running litany for Spalding. "The chances of finding his location with the tools here are low." Sam wasn't ready to risk a connection and upload his personal tool kit to a compromised system. "For tonight," he continued, "I can isolate the issues and prevent him from causing more havoc."

"Can you keep him out?"

"That requires a major upgrade for the museum. They're well-protected from the things they know about. This…" His voice trailed off until he ran into another annoying speed bump. "Well, this kid is good."

"How do you know it's a kid?" Spalding asked.

"Just an educated guess based on the language, creative approach and execution. He gained access through a gap in the contact page."

Devon and Carli added their opinions and

voices to the discussion, speculating on who was behind the attack and where they were hiding. Though Sam wasn't willing to give away the online security programs he used at Gray Box, he was happy to weave in a few improvements and lock out the hacker for tonight. "Display controls and locks are back in my control," a man said from across the room.

"The group from China will be delighted to hear it," Spalding said with obvious relief. "Almost as much as the museum director."

Sam imagined Madison would be pleased, as well. "The hard work isn't done," he warned. "This stopgap will buy the museum forty-eight hours at best. If he wants back in, he'll find a way."

"The exhibit runs through the end of the year," Madison said from over his shoulder.

Sam swiveled in the seat and met her serene gaze. "I didn't hear you come in." He checked his watch, surprised he'd been working on this for nearly an hour.

She gave him a small smile. "Can you create a solution that will last?"

"Yes, but not from here." He stood up from the workstation. "I'll work on it more tomorrow. For tonight, everything should run flawlessly."

"Wonderful." Her eyes were filled with gratitude. "Thank you, on behalf of all of us."

"We'll need to coordinate with your efforts moving forward," Spalding said. "My team needs to know what you're implementing."

Startled at the man's audacity, Sam laughed. "I'll keep you in the loop, but you're not coming anywhere near my lab at Gray Box."

"This is an ongoing FBI case," Spalding countered, planting his hands on his hips.

"All right, it's yours. What a relief I'm not needed here anymore." Sam stepped away from the workstation and shoved his hands into his pockets before he gave in to the urge to pop Spalding on the chin. At one time, he'd been a scrawny nerd. After high school, when his days were his to manage, he started putting in almost as many hours at the gym as he did at the keyboard.

"Gentlemen," Madison chided. "I'm sure we can come to terms at a more appropriate time in the morning."

Sam wanted to snarl at the insinuation that he'd cave on this point. "FBI, Department of Defense, or whoever, can sign a contract if they want a consultant. I don't work for free."

He and Rush had seen a need and gone after

it, cornering the market of online information security. They'd both developed and sold ideas for millions, so founding Gray Box hadn't been strictly a money-motivated endeavor. Although no one seemed to believe it, they had an altruistic side, professionally and personally.

Hackers once themselves, they'd been disowned by that community when they launched Gray Box. He couldn't recall a week since the company went public without an attempt on the servers. Every hacker in the world wanted the instant reputation and recognition that would come from breaking into Gray Box. The legitimate businesses they supported now still held a reserve of distrust, despite their zero-breach record. Sam reminded himself public image wasn't his problem. He left that to Rush and Rush left the lion's share of the day-to-day technology to him.

"If you're set," Sam said to Madison, "I'll be on my way." He shook hands with Carli and Devon and signed a business card for each of them. With a final nod to Spalding, he let Madison walk him out of the security suite.

"You haven't heard the last of Spalding," she murmured. "He takes his role in this seriously."

"As he should," Sam said, matching her

low tone. "I'll cooperate with him, but I'm not handing over proprietary technology or software." Again he reached to push his glasses up so he could rub his eyes and remembered in the nick of time he was wearing his contacts. "By noon tomorrow, I'll have better location intel for the FBI to work with as well as a comprehensive protective program for the museum. At a fair price."

"Remarkable." She stopped, placing a hand on his arm again. "I have one more favor to ask."

He arched his eyebrows, waiting.

She glanced up and down the hallway before meeting his gaze. "Spend a few minutes at the reception with me. News of my, *um*, husband's arrival has made people curious."

He kept her waiting, but she didn't flinch. "Okay, on one condition."

"Only one?"

He reconsidered his position. "One condition and I reserve the right to add conditions based on your answers."

She held her ground and his gaze. "I reserve the right to refuse on a per item basis. Name your primary condition."

He felt the smile curl his lips, saw her lovely

mouth curve in reply. "Tell me where and why we married."

"Not here." Her smile faded. "You deserve a full explanation and you'll get it, I promise. As soon as I navigate the minefield this evening has become. I don't have any right to impose further, but I could use a buffer in there."

He suddenly wanted to step up and be that buffer. For her. "I'm no asset in social settings, Madison."

"No one's expecting you to be a social butterfly. You only have to be yourself and pretend to be proud of me."

He didn't care for her phrasing. Before he could debate the terms further, she leaned her body close to his and gave him a winning smile. "Later," she murmured, tapping his lips with her finger. "Let's go. There's only an hour left." She linked her hand with his and turned, giving him a start when they came face-to-face with one of the guests.

Her moves made sense now. She'd known they were being watched while he'd been mesmerized by her soft green eyes. The intimacy had only been for show. Thank goodness.

If her smile was any indication, he'd managed the first introduction flawlessly. They were soon surrounded by others eager to meet Madison's elusive husband. Beside her, working the room wasn't difficult. She never left him to fend for himself and listening to her answer the same repeated questions, he learned she'd kept details of her married life private. It made the hour easier to bear.

The only thing that came naturally to him was demonstrating pride in his fake wife. She had a flare for diplomacy—no surprise, considering her career. He admired her ability to say the right things or politely evade questions she didn't want to answer.

When they entered the gallery where the prized white jade cup glowed under soft lights surrounded by guards, he was the only person close enough to catch her relieved sigh. She squeezed his hand. "Thank you, Sam. You saved me tonight."

He couldn't recall ever hearing similar words aimed at him. "We should dance," he replied, noticing other couples dancing on the terrace where live music was under way.

"You don't have to do that," she said, resisting.

This was a new role. Not the one she'd created for him with the marriage ruse, but being the eager and willing dance partner. He tipped his head to the open doors, urging her to come along. "It's a gorgeous night and it's our public debut as a couple."

"It's not necessary," she murmured as they lingered on the fringes of the dance floor.

"Afraid I'll step on your toes?" He managed to keep the growing list of questions to himself, though he couldn't wait to hear how she'd passed her security clearances with a fake husband. "Come on," he cajoled. "We deserve a little fun." Besides, he had more he wanted to say. Nothing as eloquent as the cheesy lines he'd just delivered—something far more relevant to his real reason for being here.

With a little spin, he turned her into his arms and they joined the flow of dancing couples.

"Impressive." She gave him an open, friendly smile that suited her better than the cool reserve she'd shown all evening.

"My mom was a stickler for all the traditional manners." If he focused on her, he didn't mind the other people milling about, watching them.

Madison peered up at him through her lashes. "Was that before or after juvie?"

"Both, actually," he admitted. Why conversation had always been easy with her was a perpetual mystery to him. She'd always been out of his league and yet she'd never been rude about what she needed when he tutored her. The sobering thought brought him back to the reason she'd called on him to help.

He bent his head close to hers and whispered in her ear. "There's more to the problem you had tonight, isn't there?"

Her hand smoothed a small circle across his shoulder. "Yes." The serene mask she kept between the world and her emotions fell back into place.

"I'd like to talk about it in more detail."

"As soon as I'm home I'll call you and fill you in."

"No." Based on who she was, the people around them and the disjointed threats from the hacker and online chat rooms, he didn't trust her phone or email right now. Knowing how she'd reached out to him, he had a few concerns about the security of his phone and email. "In person is better. Smarter," he added.

Her body tensed under his hands. "Sam, stop. You've done enough for me. I can handle it with the FBI's help from here."

"I'm serious, Madison." He guided her

through a turn and brought her closer to his body. "You know the history of this situation. You know the protocols and risks in your world better than I do."

When concern flared in her eyes, he knew she was following his line of thinking. If she'd used his name from the beginning of her marriage charade, he had reason to worry that his condo might be compromised. It wasn't simply his fondness for spy novels fueling the paranoia. He and Rush had survived several corporate espionage attempts, from local to global threats. As he'd watched Madison work the room, he realized several people in the Chinese delegation recognized him and were reassessing her because of it. He sensed serious trouble brewing and he needed her insight to get ahead of it.

"How long have people believed I'm your husband?"

Chapter Three

Madison knew precisely what he was asking and she was ashamed for not thinking of it earlier. Her desperate action had put *him* at risk. She blamed her oversight on being near him, close enough to touch. Holding his hand, having that strong, warm palm pressed against hers, brought her persistent fantasy to life with vivid detail. Despite the crazy twists and turns of the evening, despite knowing there were likely more problems ahead, this past hour with him had been nothing short of a dream come true.

And now she was waking up with a jolt. "Only the security clearance team is aware the wedding set is only for show." The rings had been enough of a buffer for her, until tonight.

"That doesn't answer my question," he stated, executing another perfect turn in the dance.

Of course it didn't. Sam Bellemere, master of logistics and computer code, was searching for the bug—*the flaw*—in her story. "I have no reason to believe your home has been compromised." She pushed the words through the tight smile she kept plastered on her face.

"A good start."

"I never once used your full name in any conversation or correspondence until tonight."

She felt more than heard his disbelieving snort. Did he have to push this here and now? She was worn out, had been working toward this evening for the better part of a year. She had a bottle of her favorite wine chilled and waiting at her apartment for her private celebration. "I will tell you the whole story. In person."

"I know." His hands flexed, underscoring the inevitability of those two words.

Was that a threat or a promise? Her body had an opinion, but that was nothing new. She'd worked her tail off through high school and college until finally realizing her goal of becoming a liaison with the State Department. The joy had dulled quickly when she ran up against the preconceived notions of men and women from different countries and cultures. It wasn't a shock, she knew her research, yet facing it head-on day in and day out had challenged her resolve. The illusion of having a husband smoothed out those rough edges and gave her the respect and distance she needed to excel in her position. Even the team who handled her security clearance had been on board with the idea, since there wouldn't be any issues with questionable romantic relationships.

At the office, with the people who knew her best, she'd found having a particular man in mind made the lie easier. Even if she didn't share the details of the whirlwind wedding and happy marriage, it gave her story credibility. No need to fabricate height, hair and eye color, or how her husband smiled at her over a shared joke. All she had to do was picture the man dancing with her now.

Sam Bellemere, reclusive, wealthy and brilliant, was the embodiment of her ideal husband and she had no intention of admitting such a thing. At six feet, he was the perfect height for her. His brown hair and brown eyes might sound bland, yet thinking about the flecks of gold in his irises she'd noticed when he tutored her, recalling his exasperation and amusement with her struggle to learn what he mastered so easily, always made her smile. It was those sweet memories that convinced her coworkers she'd found her soul mate.

If only it could be true.

It was impossible to ignore how he'd bulked up as he matured, filling out through the shoulders and everywhere else since high school. He was light on his feet, his muscles firm under his tuxedo. She'd read in an interview that he kept fit by boxing at a gym across town. It was obviously working.

She reeled in her attraction before it became obvious. Her crush on him had begun that first week of his tutoring. No matter where she went, who she met or dated, or how many birthdays she celebrated, he was the standard by which she measured all men. She knew being stuck on a high-school crush was ridiculous. She worried there was something wrong with her emotionally. Every attempt to break through those persistent feelings had failed.

"Madison?"

Tonight was a dream twisted within a nightmare of potential embarrassment. She'd never meant for them to play the happily married couple in public. Her body heated with every sway and step she took near him, believing the impossible. If she were brutally honest, she'd admit her entire system had gone on full alert when he stepped into the security office. Without an ice bath, she didn't stand a chance of cooling down any time soon.

"Madison?" He spun her out and back to him once more.

"Hmm?"

"What's on your mind?"

She jerked herself back into work mode. "The hacker." It wasn't really a lie. She'd mastered the art of compartmentalizing and showing interest in one thing while her mind raced off in another direction.

She really should credit that skill to Sam, as well. In high school, he'd never done more than shake her hand the first day the teacher introduced them. Her fantasies had been outrageously different. Looking back, she knew the only reason Sam's tutoring had been effective was that she'd been determined to prove she wasn't the typical dumb blonde. She wanted to earn his respect as a student and win his attention as a person. It hadn't worked, although she passed the classes she needed to keep her career goals on track. By the time they went their separate ways at graduation, she'd settled into the reality of being his friend, knowing she'd lost the chance to be his girlfriend.

"Madison?"

"Yes."

"The music's over."

Feeling the gaze of others on them, she stepped back and grinned up at him, playing the role of enamored spouse to perfection. Indulging herself, she brushed nonexistent lint from the lapel of his tuxedo so she could feel the solid muscle of his chest under his clothing. The images that flooded her mind nearly undermined her reserve and self-control.

"I need to stay until the guests are gone. Would you like me to call a car for you?"

His palm trailed down her arm until his hand engulfed hers. "Now that I'm here, I'm reluctant to leave without you."

She knew he didn't intend for those words to twine around her heart and yet she couldn't stop the response. "When did you start enjoying social outings?"

"It's a recent development." His voice, low and rough, sent a shiver of desire over her skin. With another man she'd chalk up the comment as innuendo, but that wasn't how Sam was wired.

Pulling herself together, she returned to her responsibilities of giving each guest a proper farewell and seeing everyone out of the museum as she gave more vague answers about their relationship.

Mr. Liu found her mingling with his wife and the other members of his party near the gallery and he signaled for a tray of champagne. "One last toast," he said, holding his glass high. "May the gods of happiness, wealth and longevity smile upon you both, this day and always."

They all drank to her marriage and Mr. Liu urged Madison and Sam toward the white jade cup on display while those who had arrived with him headed for the car waiting out front. "I had concerns, Mrs. Goode, as you know. Please also know I appreciate how efficiently you handled them." He slid a look at Sam.

"It is my honor, Mr. Liu," she replied. "We want you to be at ease, confident that we value the treasures you've shared here as much as China does."

Mr. Liu met her gaze with direct, pointed interest. "I find it intriguing, Mrs. Goode, that you've kept a treasure of your own so well hidden." He bowed slightly at Sam, maintaining eye contact. "Mr. Bellemere, it was an honor and good fortune to meet you personally this evening. Your company is of great interest to me."

It shouldn't have shocked her that Sam was known to leaders in China. He and Rush had established a global influence within the market of data security.

Assuming someone from the consulate hadn't tried to plant listening devices in her apartment previously, they would be desperate to do so now that she was known to be married to Sam. Mr. Liu wasn't even bothering with subtlety. If someone managed to bug her apartment, they'd soon learn she wasn't really married to Sam. Madison was calculating the fallout, the timing and how to handle it as the men chatted about computer advancements.

With no more than a glance, Sam understood what she needed and helped her guide Mr. Liu toward the car and those waiting for him.

"My son has a great interest in the computer sciences," Mr. Liu said, deftly shifting to an indirect tack. "He lacks follow-through and motivation, despite the best efforts of his family and educators. I've often thought it might motivate him to see what is possible."

"How old is your son?" Sam asked.

"Nearly eighteen," Mr. Liu replied. "He will begin at Stanford in the fall."

"A very good school," Sam said.

Mr. Liu ignored Madison's attempts to lead him down the front steps. Resigned, she watched for an opening to rescue Sam from the conversation, but Sam seemed content. She let her mind wander over the evening, considering it a success. Regardless of the invisible, contained antics of the hacker, no one had suffered a misstep or misspoken word. Except her, by calling in her fake husband to save the evening.

She owed him more than an explanation, she thought, as Mr. Liu finally joined those waiting for him in the long black limousine. With a wave, she stepped back inside, startled to find herself alone with the museum director. Had Sam decided he didn't need the full details of their fabricated marriage after all? For some inexplicable reason the idea made her sad as she and Mr. Wong chatted during the final walk-through of the museum.

When they reached the back hallway, she heard raised voices in the security office. Through the open door she saw Sam and Agent Spalding locked in a heated discussion.

"It's not something I handle so casually," Sam was saying. "You'll have to go through the appropriate channels."

"I am leading the only official investigation," Spalding fired back. "It's better for everyone if you cooperate up front."

"We don't even have an ID," Sam retorted. "Bring over a legit ID and a warrant and someone can probably tell you if he has a Gray Box. Until then you're shooting in the dark."

"Is the overnight team in place?" Madison asked Spalding, striding forward and inserting her voice into the verbal fray.

"Yes," Spalding answered, glaring over her head at Sam as if she weren't there. "The team will stay on full alert outside and in."

"Wonderful," she replied. "Then it's time for the rest of us to go home."

"You can go once I'm confident your husband will keep me in the loop."

She silenced Sam's reply with a raised finger. "He gave you his word earlier. You watched him lend us his phenomenal expertise with zero advance notice this evening. What else do you need to hear, Special Agent Spalding?"

Spalding planted his hands on his hips. "Mr. Bellemere keeps secrets for a living."

"No," Sam interjected. "My company offers people and businesses secure cloud storage solutions. That is entirely different."

"This is neither the time nor the *place*," Madison emphasized, "to get into a philosophical discussion about online privacy. I am grateful to the FBI for helping this event run safely and smoothly tonight. Whatever the hacker's goal, I'm sure we'll all work together to root him out before he causes serious trouble."

Obviously not even close to appeased, Spalding stood down for the moment. When she'd gathered her red silk shawl and her briefcase, the three of them along with the museum director walked together in a tense silence to the rear entrance of the museum. Satisfied with the alarms, Spalding offered Sam and Madison a ride. Sam refused for both of them.

"We're covered." He pointed to a limo waiting under a streetlamp on the far side of the parking lot. "My driver's waiting."

Spalding muttered something Madison didn't hear because she was nudging Sam toward the car. They had more important issues to discuss. At half past midnight, she hoped he'd let the discussion wait until morning.

The driver opened the rear door for them, giving her a small nod as she slid into the plush leather seat, followed closely by Sam. Maybe he left events with women all the time. Her heart sank a little at the thought.

When the driver was settled behind the wheel, she leaned forward to give him her address.

"Mr. Bellemere already provided the destination, ma'am," he replied.

"Thank you." She sat back and caught the grim expression on Sam's face. "What's wrong?"

He ignored her. "Jake, have you left the car alone at all tonight?"

"No, sir," the driver said. "I gassed up after I dropped you off. When I received your message, I stuck close. Didn't park until about an hour ago and no one has been near the car."

"Thank you." Sam turned the full force of his attention to her, irritation snapping in his eyes. "You can start explaining right here, right now."

"What do you mean?"

Sam's dark eyebrows arched as if her confusion baffled him. "Do I have to spell it out? The car is clean. It hasn't been left alone for anyone to tamper with."

"Tamper?" He was deliberately trying to scare her and he was succeeding.

"How often do they sweep your office for listening devices?"

She folded her arms and stared out the window. "Often enough," she said, refusing to take the bait.

"Why do they sweep for those devices?"

"Okay, point made. Stop being a jerk." She was too tired for any more diplomacy tonight. "I'm glad your limo isn't bugged. I'm sure your house isn't either."

"If we're lucky we'll catch them in the act when we arrive."

"You're being unreasonable. Wait. We?"

"It'll raise too many questions if the first time I show up to one of your events we don't go home together."

"You're overreacting." Her molars might

crack from the strain. Thoroughly exhausted, she refused to give his paranoia more fuel.

"Jake, are we being followed?"

"Always a tough call on a Friday night in traffic."

Sam grunted. "Do what you can to find out."

"Sam, I'm tired," Madison said. "I want the peace and quiet of my apartment."

"You promised me answers about this whole marriage business."

"Isn't the morning soon enough?"

"No. I'd like to hear the whole story tonight."

"Hang on." She scooted closer to him and lowered her voice. "You still don't sleep?"

He pushed a button on the console in the ceiling and the privacy screen rose between them and the driver.

Suddenly the space was far too intimate and way too reminiscent of her silly teenage-girl prom night fantasy. The illusion she'd harbored of Sam walking into the dance and taking notice of her as a girl rather than a friend. In her illusion, he'd crossed the room and kissed her right there in front of everyone. Even back then she'd known it was an impossible dream. Sam was too shy for such a public display, but she'd dreamed it anyway, night after night. Now she was a woman and she had a better understanding of what to wish for and with whom.

"Madison." His hand was gentle and warm against her bare shoulder. "Just tell me the story."

"We've been married almost two years. July Fourth is our anniversary."

"How patriotic of us," he quipped.

She tilted her head. "It came down to available time off for me, time between projects for you." She managed to play it cool until the driver suddenly took a hard right. The force dumped her into Sam's strong embrace.

"What the—"

She tried to be grateful as he righted her before she could snuggle deeper into his embrace. "He's checking for a tail," Sam explained.

"Does this happen often?"

"Rush only hires the best. You'd be surprised how many people try to hassle us."

So maybe his paranoia had stronger roots than the trouble she'd dumped on him tonight. Maybe, with a little time, he'd understand her rash actions.

"Which is my real question," Sam pressed. "Why did you choose me?"

She brought her mind back to the issue, tried

to deliver the facts in a linear, logical order. "I'm aware other cultures view single women differently, even when they're in the US," she said. "I hadn't worried much about it, but it soon became obvious I needed a polite excuse to rebuff advances. Wearing a wedding band is a common tactic, although it doesn't always stop the most persistent people." She rubbed the platinum setting on her finger with her thumb.

"What do you mean?"

She glanced up, catching a flash of anger in his brown gaze. "Possessive of a wife you just met?"

His short bark of laughter was cool, breaking the tension. "Apparently." He motioned for her to continue. "Creating a mythical husband is understandable."

"I based the myth on you." She moved her hand up and down. "Your looks, skills, all of it. Easier than creating a husband from scratch." She hoped he believed her. "I promise I never used your full name. I can't recall using your first name very often and never with anyone outside of my office."

"Why was I the foundation for your imaginary husband?"

She swallowed, too mortified to give him the truth. The car swerved again and this time Sam fell her way. His big palm landed with a delicious pressure on her thigh and she marveled that the silk didn't just evaporate under the heat.

He drew back quickly, the question lurking in his eyes.

"Because you were a friend I trusted." Because using him gave her fake husband more than an image and career, it gave him a personality. "As for tonight, the most expedient way to get you on the guest list was to own the lie and make it real. No one would question the clearance for my husband."

"Ah. Got it."

He didn't, not completely. If she was lucky, he'd never know the whole story of her ongoing infatuation with him. "Besides, you did owe me a favor."

"I'd say we flew right by even and you owe me now."

He was right and she felt terrible for it. "We don't have to keep up the ruse." She could manage things from here. "You saved the day blocking that hacker. Now you can go do your thing and I'll do mine. We don't have to play happy couple anymore."

"You're wrong about that." He drummed his fingertips on his knee.

She frowned at him. "Pardon me?" She knew the schedule and while there were several events where a date would be nice, his presence wasn't required. "I can go back to attending functions alone. It's not a big deal." After the past few hours she knew having Sam around would be the real problem because she let his presence distract her.

"I disagree. Now that I've been identified, there will be repercussions. Liu already assumes a relationship to me through you."

"He's lamenting the idea that his son is a loser who will shame the family," she said. "The topic tends to come up at every opportunity."

Sam gave her a look she remembered, the one that was part query and part disappointment in her answer. "Is the kid a loser?"

She preferred discussing a stranger to confessing her personal sins. "He's young, arrogant and entitled. That may or may not improve while he's in college."

Sam sighed, apparently satisfied. "The museum will need to stay on alert. They should also take stronger measures to shut out more hacks." He opened his mouth to say more, but the intercom beeped.

"Trouble," Jake reported.

"You know what to do," Sam replied. "Don't worry," he said to Madison.

"What trouble?" Madison twisted in her seat. The street behind them was crowded with headlights. "What does he know to do?"

Sam shrugged and she wanted to slap that smug expression off his face. "He drives a specific route we can tap into later for potential identification."

"Can he do that and then take me home?" she pleaded. "I have a meeting first thing in the morning." She wanted to get out of these heels and into her pajamas before she wrote up her report on the evening.

"On a Saturday?"

"Really?" She leaned back. "That's rich, the perennial workaholic criticizing *my* schedule."

"What happened to your famous, unflappable composure?" He patted her knee. "You pulled off a marriage charade along with mostly false assurances that an irreplaceable treasure from China is secure without batting an eye. Sitting back while my driver evades a tail shouldn't be a big deal."

She couldn't tell what he expected of her. At this hour she didn't care. "Take me home. I'll be safe in my building."

"Fake or not, tonight you're safer with your husband," he said, catching her as the driver's next turn pitched her into him again.

She couldn't control her runaway imagination. In a flash she could clearly see life as Sam's wife. It would be bliss to come home after a long day and talk with him over a pepperoni pizza and a couple of beers. Never once in her fantasy had she seen a face other than his when she thought of a husband.

Preposterous. Impossible. Wishful thinking at its finest. The car bounced a little as the driver entered a parking garage with too much speed.

"Now we're clear," Sam said a moment before Jake confirmed the status. The limousine came to a halt and Sam pushed open the door, extending a hand to help her.

Resigned to the strange turn of events, she placed her hand in his. "Where are we?"

"My place."

She glanced around at what appeared to be

an average concrete parking garage without the typical foul odors. Only five parking spaces were occupied, all of them with luxury vehicles. She recognized a sporty Porsche crossover in smoke gray and the sexy lines of a deep blue Lamborghini. She couldn't name the other three without taking a closer look. Wherever they were, the neighbors were apparently as wealthy as Sam.

Her feet ached from the high heels as he led her toward an elevator in the corner. "Sam, I really should go." If she slept without removing the heavy makeup on her face, she'd wake up looking like something from a bad horror movie. That would be mortifying and a certain end to their friendship, just in case lying about the marriage hadn't done that already. "I need—"

The elevator doors parted automatically at their approach and she glanced around for the motion sensor, forgetting her protest.

"Intrigued?" His lips twitched in a smirk. "What do you need, Madison?" he asked, pulling out his phone.

You. Thankfully, she bit back that absurd, knee-jerk response. "My apartment," she managed. "I'm sure your place is…" The elevator opened to a penthouse and the sparkling nighttime view of San Francisco stole her breath. "Oh, Sam." She couldn't stop herself from walking in, admiring everything in sight.

"You like it?"

It wasn't anything she imagined his home might be. Not the casual mess that always surrounded his work space at school. Of course it wouldn't be like that. He was a man now, a lauded expert at the top of his industry. The position obviously paid well. The furniture had a lived-in feel, modern, clean lines without feeling too stark or glossy or new. Nothing in her fantasies had prepared her for this, for seeing him in this kind of space. She could happily snuggle into the corner of that big couch next to Sam and forget there was a world out there that needed them.

Exasperated with herself, she wondered if anything would smother the torch she'd carried for him all this time. He'd never given her the first signal that he thought of her in a romantic way. Unlike his business partner, Rush, there was never a whisper of Sam having any romantic ties. Maybe that was why her heart was so stubbornly locked on to him.

She forced her gaze away from the stunning

view and faced him. "I need to go home." Staying here would be unbearable. He'd already commented on her lack of composure. "I need my space and my things."

"Let me guess?" He started typing into his phone. "Toothbrush and toothpaste. Do you still prefer that striped brand you used when we were kids?"

"Pardon me?" How did he know what brand of toothpaste she'd used in high school?

"My bathroom is surely lacking." He held out the phone to her. "Put in whatever you need and it will be here within the hour."

"No." It was closing in on one in the morning. She jerked her hands behind her back and clutched the handle of her briefcase. "No, thank you. Take me home, please."

His gaze narrowed and his brown eyes were calculating something as he studied her from head to toe. His thumbs flew over the surface of his phone and then he pocketed the device.

Before she could react to that, he'd slipped a hand around her elbow. "Take off your shoes."

"Take me home."

His jaw clenched, but his touch remained gentle. "I didn't blow your secret out of the water tonight, did I?"

"No." She tried to smile. "I appreciate that more than I can say."

"Thank me by listening for a minute. Your feet need a break from the shoes."

"You can't know that." How did he know that?

"Take them off," he said. "And follow me."

She gave in, stifling a whimper when the cool hardwood floors soothed the soles of her feet. He guided her toward the kitchen, pausing to pull out two bottles of water. He opened both and handed her one. Without a word, he continued on toward an office.

This was where he lived, she realized immediately. He enjoyed the front room, but here she saw signs of the Sam she remembered. The big corner desk with three monitors and an ergonomic keyboard was cluttered with files and books, spiral notebooks and pencils and countless small toys mixed in with various awards. His masculine scent drifted through the air.

One wall was all windows, the spectacular view currently muted by a sheer shade. In a corner was a tall, antique secretary desk, outfitted with a slim laptop, a pen and notebook and none of the clutter. A padded executive chair held a point of honor at the corner desk and a smaller version of the same chair was positioned in front of the antique.

He sat down at the corner desk and brought his computer to life. "I assume you have your own computer, but I'd rather you used the laptop over there. You can start your report while we wait for the delivery to arrive."

She barely remembered mentioning the report. Her firm boundaries crumbled with every minute she spent with him. "Sam, it's late and you're losing me." Whatever his mind had moved on to, she needed more of an explanation.

"I doubt that," he said absently. "You want to go home. I understand." He stood up and took the briefcase from her hand. "Drink your water. In a few minutes you'll see why going home is a bad idea."

She started for the opposite chair because her feet were tired, stopping short when several images popped up on his monitors. Her grip tightened on the pebbled leather of the chair's headrest as she recognized what he'd done. "You had Jake drive by a string of traffic cams when you thought we were followed."

"That's right. Rush and I worked up the protocol when we realized we couldn't rely on blind luck all the time. We were being followed," he added.

She ignored that, more concerned about the next step. "The transportation or police departments don't mind you hacking in for a look?"

"They never caught me when I did, but now I don't have to."

She didn't ask, just in case knowing the details turned her into an accomplice. She drank her water while he used various views, zooming in on the driver and passenger in the dark sedan that had tailed the limo unerringly from the museum until Jake lost them long enough to duck into the building. "Those two are part of the security force at the Vietnamese consulate. Why would they follow us?"

That brought the full weight of Sam's attention back to her. "Vietnam? You're sure?"

She nodded. "In case you haven't kept up, things are as dicey as ever between China and Vietnam. I've been working on keeping things cordial all year long."

"You didn't introduce me to any Vietnamese diplomats tonight," Sam said.

"They weren't invited to the private viewing of the exhibit. Tonight was China and America only." Had someone spilled her marriage news to someone in the Vietnamese consulate? Even if that had happened, it didn't explain being followed. "I don't understand this."

"Why work so hard to stick with us?"

She knew his query was rhetorical. Good thing, since she didn't have an answer.

"What's your address?" He tugged his tie loose and popped open the top two buttons of his shirt while he waited for her reply.

She answered, surprised by the polite question when she knew he could look it up online in seconds. It didn't take long before he'd pulled up views of street corners. He took his time while she watched over his shoulder as he searched for the car that had tailed them. "You think they're waiting for me to come home?"

"Time will tell."

At this hour speculation wouldn't get them anywhere. Even without the shoes, her feet were starting to cramp. Making a note in her phone so she wouldn't forget to bring up this detail at tomorrow's meeting, she decided that home or not, her mind and body needed rest. "Do you have a guest room?"

"Yes." Standing, he shrugged out of his tuxedo coat and folded it over the chair in front of the antique desk. "This way."

They walked through the central room, past the floor-to-ceiling windows and glorious view to the opposite side of the condo. There were two bedrooms connected by a luxurious bathroom. On the counter an array of skin care and bath products had been set out.

"Thanks," she said. It was a weak substitute for the miles of gratitude she wanted to show him. "I don't want to know how you managed this." She hadn't heard a delivery arrive or anyone moving through the condo. It was a little freaky.

"I've developed some connections through the years. You'll find pajamas and casual clothes on the bed. Hopefully something will fit. I had to guess your size." His gaze swept over her once more and her body responded with a flash of heat. "What time do you need to be at the office?"

"Weekend meetings start at ten." She nearly whined when she noticed it was just past two.

He nodded and his eyebrows came together in that familiar way whenever he crunched numbers. "That gives me some time to work. I'll make arrangements for breakfast and factor in a stop at your place."

"Great." She couldn't muster another protest

tonight. It would only fall on deaf ears anyway. "Good night, Sam." She wiggled her fingers and he left the bathroom, shutting the door on his way out. Turning to the supplies on the counter, she removed her makeup, pampered her skin and brushed her teeth, all the while wrestling with the concept of anyone having cause to follow her.

Ready for bed, she cracked the door a bit and confirmed she was alone. On the queen-size bed she found a lavender camisole, matching shorts and an oversize sleep shirt in a deeper hue. Like the items in the bathroom, everything here was brand-new. What kind of staff or assistant did he have that he could summon up toiletries and clothing with a text message in the middle of the night? Taking the tags off the sleep shirt, she stripped off her dress and lingerie. The soft cotton fabric was bliss against her skin. Pulling back the covers, she smoothed a hand over the finest sheets, wondering if Sam had chosen them or left the decision to a decorator.

Unlike most nights when she grappled with the events of the day and the uncertainties of tomorrow, Madison fell asleep within moments of her head touching the pillow.

Chapter Four

Back on what he considered his side of the condo, Sam mentally turned and flipped the various pieces of the puzzle that made up Madison Goode. If anyone had told him a woman like her would use him as a fake husband, he'd call them crazy. He had it on good authority that no woman in her right mind wanted to waste a lifetime with a man as introverted, self-involved and work-centric as Sam. He supposed he understood her reasoning for calling him *husband* about as much as she understood his extensive resources and willingness to use them for her.

Did that give them common ground or was it an insurmountable divide? "Doesn't matter," he reminded himself aloud. He'd answered the call of a *friend* and done what he could to help her. End of story.

Aside from the challenges posed by the hacker, the small, personal moments of the evening replayed in his mind as he changed clothes in his bedroom. Her small touches, the knowing looks. It had been for show, he knew that. Still, the straight, glossy hair and the shape of her legs in that killer dress had left a lasting impression. For the rest of his days, he would remember her floral perfume weaving around them as they danced.

Exasperated with his foolishness, he dumped the tuxedo in the bag for the dry cleaner and pulled on comfortable shorts and a T-shirt sporting the logo of the gym where he boxed a few times each week. He removed his contacts and slipped his glasses into place. He wasn't an evening-wear kind of man. Although he could pull it off once a year as required, he was far more content at home like this, with the company of his computers.

He sat down at his desk and started researching the people he'd met tonight. How did Madison know he didn't sleep well or often? He couldn't recall making that confession to her when they were kids. Maybe she'd picked it up from an interview, except he wasn't prone to sharing such personal details with reporters.

Pushing that distraction to the back of his mind, along with the persistent awareness that an interesting, beautiful woman was sleeping in his guest room, he turned his mind to the issues that had dragged him into her world and opened windows for several searches.

He ran a search on the car that tailed them from the museum and confirmed the registration information linked back to the Vietnamese consulate. Identifying the men wasn't his priority. Madison's recognition was enough for his needs. He printed out the information so she could take it to her morning meeting.

Setting a timer, he limited himself to another hour of research before he called it a night. He'd planned to work out an insulating layer of protection for the museum at the Gray Box offices, but leaving her here alone didn't sound like the right decision for a husband to make.

Husband. The weight and responsibility of the word settled across his shoulders, even though she was only a casual friend in truth.

He understood her explanations, especially after seeing her in action this evening. He hadn't missed the sideways looks aimed at both of them amid all the polite smiles and kind words. He fisted his hand around the pen he held, remembering the way some of the reception attendees had ogled Madison. He tossed the pen down. Good grief, he'd been a *fake* husband for a few hours and he was already possessive. He supposed it was a design flaw in his brain, reading too much into one encounter and not picking up enough of the right cues in another.

Sam tugged off his glasses and pressed his fingers to his eyes, willing himself back on track. If he wasted any more time dwelling on Madison's cover story, he'd never get any sleep. He needed to be on his toes tomorrow at the office. Though he was tempted to share the news of his "marriage" with Rush in an email or text message, his best friend deserved better.

Replacing his glasses, he picked up the pen and resumed his research into the history— recent and old—between the United States, China and Vietnam. There had to be a better motive than mere mischief to explain the hacker's timing and his choice of targets. With every layer Sam peeled back, he marveled at Madison's patience. The politics and cultural differences overwhelmed him. It was like trying to use an ever-changing set of rules to sort and read the unspoken communication among strangers at a party. Given a choice, Sam would always prefer the cut and dried logic of computers over people.

When his timer went off, he made a few notes, backed up his work on a private server and then checked the security feeds in and around his building. The team from the Vietnamese consulate had double parked across the street from the building's main garage entrance. "Nice work, guys," he muttered to the screen. His address wasn't a secret, but he didn't advertise it either.

Just over three years ago, Rush had forced him to spend more time away from the office, supposedly for his mental health. Unwilling to deal with nosy neighbors or community associations, Sam had found a building he could remodel and design to his strict, personal privacy standards. He had room here for his growing car collection as well as an entire floor where he could play with computer builds, operating systems and virus solutions, as well as develop and test new ideas.

His decision had made the city happy, Rush

happy and, most of the time, himself happy. Tonight wasn't one of those times.

For several minutes Sam watched the men in the car, debating between reporting the bad parking and sending down a couple of coffees. Yawning, he decided it wasn't time to rattle the saber. No one without a code could get into his building without tripping at least one electronic or physical alarm. Satisfied they were isolated and safe, he dimmed the lights in his office and retreated to his bedroom.

Saturday, June 11, 6:20 a.m.

SAM WOKE THREE hours later, ten minutes before his alarm sounded, with an idea for covering the gap in the museum security blasting through his brain. He went to his office, wrote it out and did a quick test. Pleased, he sent it to Rush for review.

By half past seven he'd showered and shaved and had the coffee brewing. The team in the car had gone and Sam couldn't identify any replacements. Maybe they'd given up or found answers elsewhere. So far he hadn't heard a peep from the guest room. The security system would have alerted him if she'd left. He should have confirmed the schedule for today. Then he wouldn't be standing here wondering how much time she needed to prep for her meeting.

He wished he knew how she took her coffee. When they were in school, she'd always had a Diet Coke nearby. Not an item he stocked. At their reunion, he'd seen her with a mimosa at brunch and a cosmopolitan in the evening. Maybe she didn't drink coffee at all. Rather than make another crazy list for a delivery that covered all bases, he decided to wait and ask her first.

Filling a tall mug with piping hot coffee, black as sin, he called himself out on going overboard to impress her last night. Regardless of her reasons or intentions, she'd outed them as married and he'd been compelled to put the right foundation under the illusion. Once people put his face with her ruse, they would have to follow through with the charade as a couple until they could pin down the hacker and the spotlight moved on to someone else. He'd tried to point out that fact last night and she'd avoided the topic. He couldn't give her that kind of leeway today. They had to have a plan in place before either of them left the building again.

The signal chimed that the paper had been

delivered downstairs. Although he subscribed to the online edition as well, he still liked the feel of the newspaper in his hands first thing in the morning on the weekends. He checked the security camera views from the drop-down monitor in the kitchen, then took the elevator down to the lobby to pick up the paper.

When he returned, Madison was waiting for him in the kitchen, her gaze shifting from the monitor to the elevator door. "Nice setup," she said.

"Thanks. I like it." She looked refreshed and relaxed in a casual white T-shirt and jeans, yet somehow more vulnerable without any makeup and her hair down. "Good morning."

"Is it?" She rubbed her toes up and down the calf of her opposite leg. "I've been a terrible imposition." She flicked her fingers at the monitor. "Are we still friends?"

"Yes." His reply was instant and accurate, he decided. "Absolutely." He smiled at her. "Have some coffee." He'd meant it as a question and it sounded as if he were barking orders. "Do you drink coffee?"

Her smile brightened. "Yes, absolutely," she echoed.

Changing the monitor to a local news station, he muted the sound and then handed her a mug. "I figure we have a few minutes to get our story straight before you need to dress for your meeting."

He made a mental note as she poured coffee into a mug and added a heaping spoonful of sugar. She raised the cup, breathed in the aroma and took the first sip gingerly, her eyes closed.

The sight might as well have been a sneaky left jab to the jaw. His muscles went slack for a second and then everything felt too tight as he fought for balance. He pulled out the nearest counter stool and sat down, dropping the paper onto the cool surface of the marble counter.

Her eyes popped open, her gaze locking with his. "Why don't I make breakfast?"

"I'd planned to handle that." He just needed a minute, maybe an hour, to get a grip and some perspective on what was becoming an all-too-domestic morning.

"Let me," she said. "It's the least I can do."

He chose not to argue. "Make yourself at home."

She did, pulling ingredients from the refrigerator and with his cues finding the equipment she needed for whatever she had in mind. He reviewed the headlines on the front page and tried to find the best words to broach the topics of her trouble and the ideas brewing in his head for moving forward.

"I have a security upgrade almost ready for the museum. After Rush reviews it, you and I can offer it to them at least as a trial for the duration of the exhibit on loan from China."

She shot him a look over the top of his paper. "You didn't sleep," she accused.

He'd expected a warmer reply, maybe even a thank-you. "I did too." He turned the page and flattened the paper. "How do you know about my sleep habits?"

"You mean your habit of *not* sleeping?" Her golden eyebrows puckered and smoothed out again as she smiled. "You told me once during a tutoring session." She turned back to tend to whatever she had going in the skillet. "I thought you remembered everything."

"Not exactly," he admitted, trying to recall the conversation from so many years ago and coming up blank. "What was I helping you with that day?"

"It was a test prep day," she said with a sassy grin on those natural, peachy lips. "You dozed off and on while I practiced the timed sections of Mr. Denning's midterm torture session."

Based on her expression, she seemed to remember it fondly. "Denning wasn't that bad."

She snorted. "You were his *star*. I routinely brought down the class average."

Sam grunted and picked up the next section of the paper. When she announced the two-minute warning, he set the paper aside, moved around to her side of the counter and pulled out plates, utensils and napkins for them.

He was pouring juice into glasses as she carried the skillet filled with a mouthwatering mix of shredded potatoes, bacon, cheese, peppers and eggs to the plates. Her startled cry brought him around, too late to save her from the hot skillet that landed on her foot or the plate that broke into a million sharp pieces against the slate floor.

"Sam," she gasped, hopping on one foot and pointing at the monitor. "Volume."

Whatever had set her off could wait. He scooped her up and swiveled around. Setting her on the counter near the sink, he ran cold water over her burned foot.

She hissed at the shock. "Hit the volume."

"In a minute."

She swore under her breath. At him, the mess, or the pain of the burn, he wasn't sure. He chuckled. "Is that proper language for a liaison?"

"You might be surprised," she replied. She peered past him at the mess. "Crap. I'm sorry."

He didn't care. Most days, breakfast was as overrated as sleep in his schedule. "You're more important than a little mess."

She pushed her hair back over her shoulder. "We have bigger problems anyway."

"What are you talking about?"

She jerked her chin toward the monitor and tried to slide away from him. "I need my phone. My boss is probably already calling me."

With one hand at her waist and the other just above her ankle, he kept her in place. "I'll get it. Stay here until this burn cools off."

"It's fine, Sam."

He held her with a bit more force when she tried to squirm again. It was impossible not to notice the shape of her under his palms. Only an idiot wouldn't appreciate it and Sam was frequently praised for his brilliance. "I'll give you the phone if you promise to stay put."

She agreed, though the corners of her mouth turned down into a frown. "You're bossy."

"You should've remembered that too." He relaxed when she agreed with him.

He handed her the cell phone and dealt with the mess on the floor while she made her call, checked her messages and then started in on a text or an email.

"I'm sorry," she said again. "I should be doing that."

"It's no big deal." He dumped a full dustpan into the trash and then checked her burn again. Turning off the water, he patted her foot dry with a towel and wrapped some ice in another towel. "Sit still and keep that in place for a few more minutes."

"It's better, I swear."

"What set you off?" he asked, going back to cleaning the floor.

"There were news vans outside my apartment building. The ticker mentioned a disturbance reported by residents on my floor."

"Could be anything," he pointed out. "You have lots of neighbors."

She was absorbed with her phone, likely trying to find out more through social media. "Sam, look."

He dumped the last of the broken plate and ruined food into the trash. With her foot out of the sink, he ran water into the skillet to let it soak.

Drying his hands, he took her phone and flipped through the pictures. Two policemen blocked a doorway and someone had caught an angle that showed a search going on inside. "That's your place?" he asked, half-afraid he knew the answer.

When she didn't reply, he glanced up to find her face had paled. "Why would a disturbance lead them to search my apartment?" she wondered aloud.

He tilted her phone so she could see it. "That's Spalding, right?"

She nodded, her soft green eyes full of worry. "I have to get over there."

"Not yet and not alone," he said.

"Sam, I have to change clothes before my meeting. I'm sure they'll want a statement."

"Probably. What can you tell them? Better to go in armed with information," he said. "Do you have a security system?"

She tilted her head. "Kind of. It's a passive nanny-cam setup."

"It's a start."

She checked her phone again, then turned it to him to show him the status on the app she used. "The cameras have been disconnected, but I have the feed linked to a Gray Box. I just need to log in to that or sync the apps."

"There's some good news. Log in is better," he said. He could get a better timeline and idea of the problem by accessing her building security. There was a decent chance he could manage that from his home office. If not, he could definitely do it on-site. "I doubt Spalding would let you in there right now."

Her hands fisted at her sides. "It's my place."

At the moment it appeared to be the FBI's place. He wisely kept the opinion to himself. "Whatever happened overnight, you have a rock-solid alibi with me. Your husband," he added to drive the point home.

She rolled her eyes to the ceiling.

"You also have our driver as well as an entire series of traffic-cam confirmation of our whereabouts between the museum and here."

"Right." She pulled her hair up and back, resting the bundle and her hands on top of her head. "I just need to think."

"We need information," he said. He plucked her from the counter and carried her out of the kitchen, her hair cascading over his arm in a wash of lemon-scented silk.

"I'm not an invalid, you know."

He knew. "There could be bits of glass on the floor. Your feet have been through enough."

"Fine." When she was steady on her feet, he refilled their coffee mugs and added sugar to hers.

She arched an eyebrow. "Ever the quick study."

"May good habits never change." His gut told him she needed a fast problem-solver as well as the illusion of a husband to unravel this mess.

His system chirped an alert at the street level and he groaned when he recognized the car. The camera showed Rush behind the wheel and Lucy in the passenger's seat. He glanced at the clock. "Is your meeting mandatory?"

"Yes."

"Call your boss again." He jerked a thumb to the monitor. "You're going to be late."

He should have sent that heads-up text about the marriage charade after all. Sam knew the coming encounter was inevitable; he only wished they could have had the discussion man to man first rather than as couples. It was shaping up to be a long day.

Chapter Five

Despite her lack of professional attire, Madison wrapped herself in her calm, all-business, State Department attitude as soon as the elevator doors parted. Rush Grayson and his new wife, Lucy, stepped into the condo in a cloud of happy good-morning greetings. Their gazes skipped over Sam and unerringly locked on to her. This might have been a planned breakfast Sam forgot, though Madison didn't believe it. The overbright smiles didn't mask the underlying concern. She felt like a bug under a microscope.

A bug wearing clothing that wasn't even hers, she thought, fighting a bout of nerves. She laced her fingers at her waist, subtly covering the wedding set she forgot to take off last night.

Rush, in a red polo shirt, khaki shorts and deck shoes, carried a large picnic basket. Beside him, Lucy beamed. She wore a strappy, pale green sundress and had a straw tote looped over her shoulder. Her summery sandals coordinated with the tote and she practically glowed with contentment. Madison stifled the reactive spike of envy for the shoes and the couple.

They might be dressed as if they'd stopped in on their way to the bay for a day of sailing, or whatever billionaires did on Saturday mornings, but Madison knew they'd popped in unannounced to protect their friend. How had they heard about last night? Braced for the worst, she knew diplomacy would be the word of the hour when explaining her sudden presence in their friend's life.

When the basket and tote were set aside on the countertop, Sam startled her by drawing her to his side for introductions. He quietly emphasized Madison's role in getting Rush and Lucy out of the jam in France just before Christmas. Instantly, the tight smiles relaxed into relief and courteous handshakes turned to warm hugs. She took it all in stride, politely giving Rush and Lucy her full attention when she wanted to check her phone for missed calls, emails and news updates.

"Well, we brought champagne," Lucy declared with another warm smile. "And orange juice in case you were out, Sam."

"Champagne?" He frowned in confusion, his gaze darting from Lucy to Rush. Then he grinned, his dark eyebrows arching high. "You're pregnant?"

"No," Lucy replied, exchanging a confused glance with her husband. "We wanted to toast your marriage." She shot a look at Madison's left hand and the wedding rings still on it.

"Since we weren't invited to the ceremony," Rush added pointedly.

Madison had opened her mouth to tell them the truth when Sam spoke up. "I was planning to stop at the office later today and fill you in." He slid his arm around her waist. "We've kept it quiet for some time now."

"Really?" Rush arched an eyebrow. A wealth of doubt dripped from the single word. "Why would you do that?"

"It's complicated," Sam hedged.

Madison shifted enough to catch his attention. Why was he duping his friends? "How did you hear the news?"

Lucy, unloading the tote, held up the society page from the morning paper. "We brought you an extra copy, in case you wanted to frame it or something."

Madison wanted a hole to open up and swallow her as she stared at the pictures under the headline: Is Another San Francisco Most Eligible Bachelor Off the Market?

The collage of incriminating photos strung together with speculation and clever quips took up half the page. Her stomach churned with guilt. Sam would hate this kind of exposure. There was a shot of him under the bright lights of a hotel leaving the event alone and a picture of him walking up the block to the museum. The photographers had caught shots of them dancing at the gala and a grainy image of them in the museum hallway, her finger to his lips. How had they caught that? The article finished with a picture of the final toast Mr. Liu had offered, along with the purpose for it. Oh, she should have seen this coming. No photographer would turn down a chance to broadcast billionaire Sam Bellemere turning up married. This was her fault.

"You're very photogenic," Sam noted, giving her waist a friendly squeeze.

"Tell them," she murmured through clenched teeth. The smile he gave her, packed with shared secrets, set something aflame deep in her belly.

"Let's save the champagne for later." Sam set out fresh mugs and poured coffee for each of them. "Did you bring food?" he asked, eyeing the basket. "We had a small breakfast mishap."

"We brought half a dozen maple glazed bacon doughnuts from the kiosk near the boathouse," Lucy said. "Along with half a dozen of the chocolate rose they had today." Rush took the bags of doughnuts to the low coffee table between the sofas flanking the stunning view and Lucy brought a stack of paper plates and napkins.

With her coffee cup in hand, Madison tucked one foot under her and curled into the corner of the couch. If Sam understood her signal to distance himself from her, he was blatantly ignoring it, sinking into the cushion next to her.

Wasting no time, she launched into the explanation of why she'd listed their friend as her husband on the guest list last night. "I should have found another solution. You all have my apologies."

"I'm not surprised the staff wasn't up to a hacker, but I'd expect better from the FBI," Rush said with a frown, ignoring the husband detail entirely. "The government keeps telling us we're not needed when Gray Box bids on contracts."

Lucy patted his knee and spoke to Madison. "The wedding set is lovely. Do you always wear it?"

"She does," Sam answered. "Helps her ward off the unwanted advances. You should see the jerks that come to these things," he added for Rush.

"I can imagine," Lucy said with a sympathetic glance.

"It had never been necessary to use more than a first name with my coworkers," Madison explained. "Until last night, no one ever knew the Sam I mention was Sam Bellemere." It sounded more ridiculous with every telling. "I never expected Sam to be forced into the spotlight this way."

He rolled his shoulders and took a sip of coffee. "I owed you."

"We all owe you, Madison," Rush agreed.

"Taking care of the hacker more than covered any perceived debt." She hated the formality in her voice. "I know I overstepped and put you in a bad spot," she said to Sam.

"It might be too soon for past tense. I'm not so sure we've taken care of him." Sam leaned forward, bracing his elbows on his knees. "Did you look at what I sent over this morning?"

Rush nodded. "I figured we could discuss it here once we sorted out your marital status."

"Married." Sam's gaze caught hers and held. Then he winked at her. "We tied the knot in Las Vegas, on July Fourth almost two years ago. I forced it into the public records last night while I was doing research."

"You hacked the State of Nevada?" Rush demanded.

"Only one database," Sam confirmed. "No biggie."

Rush swore and Madison jumped to her feet and Lucy sat back, laughing merrily at all of them. "What did you expect him to do?" she asked her husband. When Rush merely swore again, she put the question to Madison.

"I, *um*. I don't know." What had she expected? "Definitely not that." She stared down at Sam. "You were supposed to be done with the illegal access stunts." At his shrug, she planted her hands on her hips.

"Rewind a minute," Rush said, settling back to the sofa. "What did you mean about too soon for past tense?"

"The more I dig, the more I think last night's hacker is up to more than he seems." Sam patted the cushion beside him. "Sit down, Maddie. We can fight over whether or not I'm reformed later. I need you back in full diplomat mode right now."

Maddie? He'd made it sound like an endearment. She shook her head as she resumed her seat, pressing herself back into the corner of the couch to do as he asked. "I'm listening."

"The hacker clogged up a chat room with threats against the exhibit and a few people at the Chinese consulate," he explained to Rush and Lucy. "Petty stuff, easy to see through unless you're looking at it with FBI-colored glasses." Sam gulped down more coffee. "And messing with the exhibit was nothing more than showing off his access to the systems."

"You think he'll strike there again?" Lucy asked.

"If the museum installs what I worked up, the people and exhibits will be fine. The tracking program will eventually expose his location, which helps everyone in the long run."

"What aren't you saying?" Madison asked.

Again, Sam addressed Rush. "We were tailed back here by two men Madison recognized from the Vietnamese consulate. Today, her apartment is breaking news while the FBI conducts a search after a disturbance last night. The reasoning isn't clear yet." He reached over and covered her knee with his hand. "I think you're being used and your apartment is one piece in an elaborate mousetrap that was sprung last night. Exposing our secret marriage, coming here, may have saved your life. The hacker had every reason to think you'd go home to your apartment after the event."

The implication shocked her. He had to be exaggerating the threat, but she didn't want to say so in front of his friends. The one thing she understood was the need for clear facts and more of them. "No one has any reason to kill me."

"The Vietnamese security team followed *us*," Sam repeated, as if she needed the reminder. "They knew you were here with me all night, since they staked out the building until dawn."

Madison clutched her coffee cup in both hands. "I thought your driver lost them."

"It's not *impossible* to find out where I live, just challenging," he said. "I certainly wasn't the only one with a busy cell phone last night." He jerked a thumb back to the newspaper on the counter. "The proof is how fast news of our marriage hit the paper. We need to keep up the appearances of wedded bliss for your safety."

Last week, spending time with Sam would have been a dream coming true. She knew acting this out as husband and wife would strain their friendship. When she sent out his email Christmas card this year, he'd probably delete it unread. This could even be the year he didn't send her a card in return. The thoughts weighed heavily on her mind as she searched for a solution that would give him a graceful exit from this mess.

"You think the hacker is from China?" Rush asked Sam.

"That can't be," Madison interjected. "No one from China would have risked harming the white jade cup, not even to make a point."

"A rival, then," Rush suggested. "Is someone trying to make Madison a scapegoat or something?"

"In light of the search at her apartment, I think we have to consider that possibility,"

Sam said. "Whatever is going on," he continued, turning to her, "we need to get ahead of this before the hacker drops the anvil on your head."

"What do you mean?" She heard the tremor in her voice and ordered herself to stay calm.

"I admit it's not much more than guesswork right now," Sam began. "You're surrounded by some serious problem-solvers. Together the four of us are better than any one of us alone. Can you explain how you're familiar with the hacker who struck last night?"

"Familiar is overstating it," she said, resigned and frustrated. "There have been several small computer glitches and hack attempts at the office in the past six months." At Sam's hard look, she tallied them. "Five. There have been five small attacks. The first one came on the Vietnamese New Year when a spam virus ripped through our email system. Nothing sensitive was compromised, just pesky little annoyances. Aside from that, our cyber security team deals with the usual attempts to break down the firewall. Naturally our office is very careful about what devices we use, the classified statuses and how it's all backed up."

"Understandable," Rush said.

Sam was frowning. "Have you told anyone at your office you recognized the group hacking the chat room last night?"

She sipped her coffee, letting the liquid soothe her throat. "I had to treat the threat as credible," Madison said. "When we compared screenshots from the chat room to the previous emails and compared the vocabulary, I knew the personal threats were bogus."

"How?" Rush and Sam asked in perfect unison.

"I picked up a few things when he was my tutor." She tipped her head toward Sam. "In the screenshot, I saw one line of code that repeated and called Sam in rather than call off the gala."

"That sounds like a big risk," Rush said.

Madison set her coffee on the table and sat back again, folding her hands in her lap. "It was easier to make that call knowing the extent and professionalism of the security team on-site. I've been in constant contact with the museum staff while they prepared for the exhibit. None of the security cameras inside or out showed signs of tampering. It seemed to me that theft wasn't the goal, embarrassment was. I quickly determined we could and should proceed."

On the table, her cell phone rang. "My boss," Madison said. "He'll be furious I'm late." She excused herself to the guest room to answer the call.

Her boss, Charles Vaughn, replied to her immediate apology with a whisper. "Where are you?"

Considering Sam's speculation, she reworded her answer. "I'm at my husband's condo. Didn't you get my message?"

"No. Where is your laptop?"

"Here with me."

"That's a plus. Don't turn it on." Charles sighed heavily. "They all have GPS tags and I need you to lie low for a while. The reason Special Agent Spalding searched your apartment was that he received an anonymous tip that you've taken payoffs to influence the players in the South China Sea."

First horror and then outrage funneled through her veins. "That's absurd," she managed through gritted teeth. Even if she had that kind of influence, she wouldn't risk her career and reputation by selling out.

"I know. Spalding won't give me any details.

Legal is working on it. They advise you to avoid any publicity or public outings for now."

"You're telling me to hide."

"Yes," her boss said. "Having a billionaire husband is your best defense against the presented motive right now. Do not access any office files or connect to our network."

"I'm innocent," Madison protested. She wanted to deal with the trouble head-on. "Spalding knows me. He must have doubts about this tip."

"He wouldn't move on unsubstantiated rumor," Charles said.

Her boss was right. She knew Spalding's reputation. The tip must have given the FBI something solid for them to leap into action so quickly. A chill swept over her skin. "Who does the tipster claim paid me off?"

"Spalding hasn't shared that with me. If it looks credible, he has to follow all the steps," Charles reminded her. "You know how this goes. Take some of that vacation time you've built up. Let your husband take you to Hawaii and have a real honeymoon."

She snorted. They both knew leaving town for something as simple as a day trip to Monterey would make her look guilty. "If I do that now, it's as good as a confession."

"Help me out here," he insisted. "Protect yourself. The apartment search on the news is trouble enough. Once the reasons for the move come out, if you're in the office, the consulates will be in an uproar."

Right again. Still, she fought against the unfairness of it all. "I didn't do anything wrong."

"I know. I'll have Legal contact you through your husband," he said. "It's the best way to keep you off the radar."

She cringed at that. "Yes, sir."

When the call ended, she stared at her cell phone long after the screen faded to black. So much for dodging the anvil Sam mentioned. She was off the radar all right. In Sam's private fortress, her only possessions were rumpled eveningwear, her phone and a laptop she couldn't open without the risk of serious repercussions.

Knowing how Sam valued his privacy, she hated trampling all over it. She glanced at the red mark on her foot. Under the burn a bruise was swelling, a fraction of what it might be without his first aid. She'd screwed up breakfast, the one nice thing she'd tried to do for him.

Worse, if he kept being so understanding about her intrusion, if he kept touching her and caring for her, she might explode from pent-up desire. She dropped her phone to the bed and went to the bathroom to splash her face with cool water.

He was too decent for his own good. Far too decent for her after the predicament her lies had created. Good grief, he'd nearly lied to his best friends about the fake marriage she'd concocted. If there had been a time in her life when she'd been more upset with herself, she couldn't remember it now.

At the knock on the door, she turned to see Lucy smiling at her. "The guys have switched to a geek language I don't want to understand. I told them I'd check on you. Are you okay?"

"I didn't mean for this to get out of hand." Tears of frustration clogged her throat. "It was lazy of me to call him my husband when a little extra legwork and a few calls would've gotten him into the reception."

Lucy walked over and handed her a tissue from the box on the counter. "There are times when we're forced to do things in ways that aren't comfortable." She patted Madison's shoulder. "Was your boss terribly upset?"

Madison frowned at her reflection as she blotted her eyes and nose. "Sam's right that someone is targeting me. Rather than go in to the office and discuss it, I'm to stay off the radar." She snorted a sardonic laugh. "I want to fight and my boss suggested taking a honeymoon. I promise you, Lucy, if I could get out of Sam's life this instant I would." She turned her back on her blotchy reflection. "I'll find another option and let him have his privacy back."

Lucy smiled gently. "I hope that's not true." She picked up the full-size box of makeup remover towelettes. "Do you like these?"

"They worked really well last night," Madison admitted. "Why?"

"I've never seen this bathroom stocked beyond hand soap. My guess is a woman planning to invade a billionaire would have packed travel sizes of her favorite things."

"It wasn't my idea," Madison said quickly. "Sam insisted I stay here. He wouldn't let me go home after we were followed. Somehow he managed to get all of this delivered in the middle of the night. Clothes too. Come look."

She showed Lucy the pile of clothing she'd moved from the bed to the chair so she could sleep. The memory, along with the illogical upheaval of the last eighteen hours, brought a burst of laugher out of her. "Does he keep a personal shopper on retainer?"

"Yes." Lucy chuckled at Madison's shock. "It began as a business investment. You should ask him about it sometime."

A personal shopper on retainer. The concept wasn't new; it was the twenty-four-hour access and instant delivery that boggled Madison's mind. She had no intention of prodding Sam about his investments.

"Sam enjoys spoiling his friends," Lucy said, shaking her head at the obvious overkill.

"In my experience he enjoys extending his generosity from a distance," Madison said. "I'll think of another solution," she said again. "You don't have to worry about me abusing his hospitality."

"Hmm." Lucy wandered over to the bedroom window. "Do you think that's why we came over? To protect him?"

"Didn't you?"

"We were concerned," Lucy confessed. "Sam is so shy and the paper didn't mention his reason for being at the museum reception." She sank onto the window seat and pleated the flowing fabric of her dress between her fingers. "I think you'd offend him if you bailed out now."

Madison flopped back on the bed and stared at the ceiling. Lucy was right. Sam had gone the extra mile for her, from defeating the hacker at the exhibit to making sure the record of their marriage held up. Rush and Lucy stopping by might have caught him off guard, but Sam, true to his nature, had anticipated the potential fallout of her lie.

"I don't handle 'helpless' well," Madison admitted.

"Want my advice?" Lucy asked.

"Sure." She didn't move.

"I say we hand over any electronic devices to Sam and Rush and go have a girls' day. I think I should get to know the woman who is effectively my sister-in-law."

"Fake sister-in-law," Madison clarified, sitting up to better study Lucy.

"You're not saying the society section is wrong, are you?" Lucy's dark eyebrows arched in comic horror. "Come on, sis. Today is a day to exert some feminine power. Nothing says crisis management like a girls' day."

Madison offered logic, the only argument she had left. "Girls' day doesn't sound like an off-the-radar event."

"Have a little faith." Lucy grinned. "Are you in?"

At Madison's agreement, Lucy pulled out her phone. She sent several messages and then beamed at Madison. "Let's go run it by the tech twins."

Madison found herself up against an immovable force in Lucy. She carried her briefcase back to Sam's office and let Lucy deliver the plan to the men. She was more than a little awestruck as Lucy conquered each argument. To her surprise, Lucy already had confirmation from a massage therapist and an aesthetician that they would be at the Grayson boathouse by noon.

"Come on. You know the security setup. We'll be safe inside all day," Lucy promised for the third or fourth time. "Not anywhere in public view." She swatted away another protest from Sam as confirmation for lunch came in from a restaurant. "Shall I schedule dinner at our place?" she asked with an overdose of sweet innocence. "Or at the office?"

"Office," Sam said, seizing on the option. "We'll head that way in my car within an hour. That way, if the FBI or anyone else is watching this building it should throw them off."

"I doubt they can get a warrant for this building, but we know there's no cause to search the offices," Rush added. "Excellent plan," he said to his wife.

"I do have them once in a while," she replied with a grin, leaning into him for a quick kiss.

The flirty, relaxed manner went against everything she'd heard about Sam's business partner. Oh, he had a reputation as a playboy—before Lucy. The obvious contentment and easy happiness between them was something the press and paparazzi never adequately captured.

"Are you sure it's safe to open my laptop at all?" Madison didn't want to risk her problems creating a blowback on Sam or Gray Box. "It has a GPS chip."

"Let them worry about that," Lucy replied before Sam could open his mouth. "We need to get moving." She tugged Madison out of Sam's office and blew Rush a kiss. "Bye, love."

He came out of his chair at lightning speed and pulled her into his arms for a proper farewell kiss that left Madison blushing. Feeling Sam's gaze on her, she studiously avoided eye contact.

"Stay out of trouble," Rush said. "Both of you."

With only her driver's license, her State Department ID and a lip gloss in the beaded clutch she'd carried last night, Madison didn't have enough technology to get into any trouble.

Sam was scowling at her anyway. "Hang on."

Her heart gave a hopeful zing that he might kiss her. Instead he walked right by her to the coat closet tucked into the corner near the elevator. "Here." He handed Madison a zippered hoodie and a Gray Box ball cap. "Put those on."

The jacket nearly swallowed her and it smelled like him—sunshine and oceanside cliffs. She had to stifle the urge to bury her nose in the fabric. "Thanks."

"Do you have sunglasses?"

"Not with me."

"She can use mine." Lucy ushered her through the motion-activated elevator doors and down to the same parking level where Jake had dropped them off last night.

"Is the building newly renovated?" Madison asked. "I'm surprised there aren't more tenants."

Lucy gave her a long, speculative look as they walked down the row to Rush's Tesla. "Sam didn't tell you he owns the building?"

Madison shook her head. "We haven't had many normal conversations." That explained the sparse garage. Sam would be extremely choosy about who he allowed into the building.

In the driver's seat, Lucy started the car and pressed the code to exit the building. "Sunglasses," she said, pointing to a pair hanging from the visor.

"Thanks."

The car glided almost silently toward the exit. "Rush told me he forced Sam to get a place away from the office when they moved into the new building. Being such an introvert, he bought a building and renovated to his specs. He's the only tenant."

Madison glanced back, though they'd turned the corner and she couldn't see the building any longer. "All those cars are his?"

Lucy nodded. "As far as I can tell, the cars are his only hobby beyond his computers."

Madison thought he'd held his own last night, as if being an extrovert and meeting new people came naturally. "No one would've guessed how shy he is at the party last night," she said, feeling miserable all over again for putting him through that ordeal. "He greeted everyone, danced and chatted as if he went out every weekend."

"You're kidding." The utter disbelief on Lucy's face exacerbated Madison's guilt.

"Rush and I didn't even see him leave the fund-raiser. The next thing we know, his face is plastered on the society pages next to yours. He did look happy in those pictures."

So he'd become a better actor since high school. Good for him. "He enjoyed shutting down the hacker," Madison said.

Lucy sputtered out a laugh. "Maybe that's how we'll get him out of the office more often."

"Why does it bother you that he's always in the office in the first place?" It dawned on Madison that his friends seemed to be pushing him out of his comfort zone consistently. She gave in to the need to defend him. "He loves his work and he's brilliant at it. He stays fit and sharp. It's not like he's wasting away or anything."

"Oh, I like you a lot." Lucy bounced a little in her seat. "We're going to have a great time today."

Hiding under Lucy's sunglasses and Sam's sweatshirt and ball cap, Madison wasn't as convinced. Although she couldn't argue that Sam's closest friends cared about him, she wondered if anyone really knew the man who'd so easily rescued the exhibit from disgrace and stepped in to give her lies substance when he could have easily walked away.

In some ways, his consistent concern for her surprised her more than the car collection, the refurbished building and the twenty-four-hour personal shopper. From her vantage point, he'd more than fulfilled the favor owed. The way he kept sticking his neck out for her amplified her crush on him. She'd had it bad before, but now, assuming she got out of this current mess, no man would ever measure up to Sam's standards.

Chapter Six

In the back of his mind, Sam kept track of the schedule Lucy had outlined. He and Rush had been alone no more than ten minutes before they took Madison's phone, State Department laptop and the doughnuts downstairs to the lab he'd built when he refurbished the building. Knowing the women were fine, he breathed a sigh of relief when Rush shared the text message and a picture from Lucy when they were safely behind the armed security system of the boathouse.

Sam shook his head at the instant camaraderie. In the picture, the women grinned as if they'd been friends for decades rather than an hour or two.

When his stomach rumbled, he reached for another doughnut. He thought of the hearty breakfast Madison had prepared and he worried about her. She must be famished after running on a smidge of sleep, a jolt of caffeine and the sugary doughnut chaser. Last night was proof that her career kept her hopping, but he'd held her close enough to know she was in the kind of shape that resulted from taking excellent care of herself.

"You sure you want to do this?" Rush watched Sam from his place at a computer where he was putting the new software for the museum through another test.

"I understand if you want some distance," Sam replied. "Why not take the Lamborghini and head over to the office?"

Rush whistled. "With that kind of offer, I have to assume you want me gone."

"What?" Sam looked up from his study of Madison's phone and blinked a couple times to bring Rush's face into focus. "Stay or go. It's your call." He took a bite of the doughnut before he started protesting too much. "You could go work your charm on the museum, though. If we can interrupt the circling sharks, maybe we can narrow down this situation."

"Let's go through it again, then," Rush said. Together, they reviewed the program and the embedded code that would track the hacker if he struck again. When they were satisfied it was fully functional, Rush made the call and set the installation appointment for just after the museum closed tonight. "Do you want me to handle it or send someone else?"

"I think it sends a stronger message if you and I go together," Sam replied.

"It might, except her boss told her to spend time with her husband. How will it look when you decide to work instead of cozy up with her?"

Sam cringed, for reasons other than the obvious. Rush was right and the last thing Madison needed was for her husband to appear to leave her alone. "Fine. You handle the program install." He pulled a flash drive from his pocket. "Install this too."

Rush gave the small device a wary glance. "Will I regret it?"

"No more than we regret juvie," Sam answered.

"Yeah, but we can take any of those punks now."

Sam laughed with his best friend. "We won't regret it. It's a simple filter to let me monitor specific problems from here. Only the code I need to see will show up."

"I was kidding." Rush clapped him on the shoulder. "I trust you, man."

"Thanks."

Sam was downloading all the apps and programs from Madison's phone for analysis, his mind struggling with who had taken aim at her and why. "She called me while my phone was off last night," he said, mostly to himself. "I almost didn't call her back. I was tired of being on display."

"And you're wrestling with the what-ifs," Rush said quietly. "What do you think would've happened if you hadn't gone over to help?"

Rush knew him too well. The hair at the back of Sam's neck stood on end. He didn't want to think about her being ogled by diplomats with only a wedding set as a shield. He didn't care for the idea of her being tailed home by men from another consulate. She probably wouldn't have noticed until it was too late. He'd studied her apartment building and knew she would've been vulnerable before too long.

"Do you remember her at all?" he asked.

"I remember you complaining about the

tutoring to fulfill your community service."
Rush boosted himself up on one of the long
worktables littered with cables, fractured elec-
tronics and various tools. "What a whiner. I
had hours of janitorial work."

"Same thing," Sam joked. "No one cared
about how I could help, except Madison. She
needed better grades in the upper-level math
and comp-sci classes to stay competitive and
Denning had no use for her. She worked her
ass off with me."

"Sounds like she liked you," Rush said in a
goofy singsong voice.

Sam leaned back in his chair. "We got along
okay."

"You're oblivious," Rush muttered. "Come
clean with me. Why in the hell are you really
going all out with the husband routine?" He
stopped and his eyes narrowed. "Unless you
want to. That's it, isn't it?"

"Shut up," Sam barked. "It's not like that.
She cleared the fib with her security clearance
team and would never have given my full name
until last night forced her hand."

"Uh-huh." Rush folded his arms and waited.

"On second thought, I'll work better alone
today." Sam turned his back on his friend.

"Give me a break." Rush walked over, lending moral support as Sam opened Madison's laptop. "You're going above and beyond and you know it."

When the system asked for it, Sam inserted Madison's department identification card into the reader. "I'm not so sure. Her world isn't at all what I expected."

"What does that mean?"

Aware of the GPS and her boss's orders not to turn on the laptop, Sam took precautions to hide his investigation from the State Department and FBI. Once he was convinced they were in the clear, he immediately started duplicating the hard drive. "It was a private reception and viewing at the gallery. Only the Chinese and the American diplomats were invited. A few people from China recognized my name and made a couple of awkward insinuations."

Rush swore. "We do have a global clientele. What kind of insinuations?"

"That's just it." Sam sat back while the systems worked. "The comments could have been small talk. Possibly, one diplomat from China extended an invitation to a conversation I don't want to get tangled up with. There was even a veiled query about mentoring one of his kids," he said with a shrug. "You know me. I might have read too much into it. Regardless, I played off the comments as generous compliments and kept moving through the room."

"You working the room," Rush said. "What a concept."

Sam ignored that and started picking apart the hard drive, searching for anomalies in Madison's typical computer behavior. Rush pulled up a stool and sat down beside him, helping him make notes to explore and expand on when they returned to the Gray Box offices. They wouldn't connect Madison's computer to the servers there unless it was clean and only once they were sure the connection wouldn't drag them into this mess.

"Did you recognize the hacker's signature?" Rush asked after an hour.

"No one using that signature has made an attempt on our encryption," Sam replied. "One of the first things I checked." He pointed Rush to a secondary file he'd created last night to further protect their business interests. "I figured if the Chinese diplomats knew me, it wouldn't be long before the hacker learned who'd ended his party early."

"Always anticipating," Rush said.

"That's why we split the big bucks," Sam murmured, lost in his evaluation of Madison's email correspondence. When they finally had a log of the data patterns he wanted, he shut down her computer.

"Ready for me to call a driver and take this to the office?"

Sam pushed his glasses up his forehead and pressed his fingers to his eyes. Glasses back in place, he checked the cameras overlooking the street outside the building. "We've got company again," he said, pointing to the sedan at the corner. He ran the plates to be sure. "Not the same crew as last night. Why don't we use public transit? I doubt anyone watching us is prepared for that move."

Rush agreed and they made a plan to divide and conquer the team on the street. Although his appointment wasn't until this evening, Rush wanted to visit the museum earlier and see the galleries and flow. There were both straight and convoluted routes by cable car or bus from Sam's building to both the museum and the Gray Box offices in the heart of the financial district.

"As long as we grab lunch first," Rush said as his stomach rumbled.

They walked a block from Sam's building to his favorite deli around the corner. Rush sent a text message, checking on Lucy and Madison, while they waited for their order. With a remote connection to his building system, Sam kept an eye on the men tailing them. Seeing the picture of Rush's boathouse turned into a shopping boutique eased another layer of Sam's tension. At least Madison would be effectively distracted.

"You're not as pissed as I thought you'd be," Rush observed after they were settled at a high-top table with thick-stacked roast beef sandwiches and a couple of beers.

"You mean about the hacker?" Sam snagged a homemade potato chip from the basket between them and dipped it in mayonnaise.

"No." Rush glared at him. "About the *woman*."

Why wouldn't Rush drop this? "She's a good friend."

"As far as the world is concerned, she's now your *wife*," Rush said. "Have you even called your mom?"

Sam had to work to swallow the food that

had turned to sawdust in his mouth. "Forgot that," he admitted. "I'll call her as soon as we get to the office."

"Bet she's furious," his best friend said with a smirk.

Sam's mood brightened suddenly with another memory. "Bet she isn't." His mother had been a major proponent of the tutoring program and had even met Madison once. It had been a rainy afternoon and Madison's ride was late, so she waited in the car with Sam and his mom. "Mom might've suggested I ask Madison out."

Rush snorted. "And she won't be at all surprised it took you more than a decade to do it. Still, I've got fifty bucks that she'll read you the riot act before she pops any champagne."

"You're on." Sam knew better than to believe he had much grace time before his mother caught wind of his marriage. If his face wasn't all over the society page, he might've had a chance. The fact that he hadn't sent so much as a text proved how much Madison's trouble preoccupied him. He never had been able to let go of a good puzzle once he had his teeth in it. Madison's work and her current predicament were definitely a puzzle he wanted to solve and fast.

Rush's eyebrows arched in shock. "I want proof."

"Fine." Sam grabbed another chip. "I'll put the call on speaker for you."

"Nice." A gleam of triumph flashed in Rush's eyes. "Will you tell her the whole story?"

"No way," Sam admitted.

"So you'll let her believe you got married in secret?"

Sam bit off a big chunk of his sandwich as a stall tactic. He'd been working on it since last night and still couldn't find a good answer for why he'd gone along with Madison's story so easily. If the friend line wasn't enough for Rush, it would fall well short of the explanation his mom deserved.

"The best way through is through, right?" he said at last. It had been their mantra in juvie when surviving came down to the two of them against other kids far bigger and meaner. "We'll figure it out."

Rush's mouth fell open. "You're seriously playing it out."

"May as well." Sam shrugged and took a deep drink of his beer. He didn't know how things would end up, only that he wouldn't leave Madison to cope with this alone. "She needs a friend." Too bad he wasn't thinking entirely platonic and friendly thoughts about Madison. When he wasn't researching the players or evaluating the code options, his mind drifted to decidedly more intimate areas. He knew how enticing it felt to dance with her. What would it be like to kiss her, to sift his hands through that golden hair, or to have her body under his?

Rush waved a hand in front of his face. "Sam? Pretending doesn't make it real."

"Just drop it," Sam said, a low growl in his voice.

"Crap." Rush snatched the basket of chips out of reach. "You want to keep her. You deserve a better relationship than a convenient accident," he insisted. "When will you stop being such a coward?"

"Shut up." He would *not* take this from Rush, of all people. "You've got no room to talk. Lucy *ran away* from you."

Rush's eyes narrowed. "She came back."

Sam snorted. They both knew Lucy came back into Rush's life because she'd been blackmailed. Somehow the two of them had made

it work, but Sam didn't need this level of hy-
pocrisy out of his best friend.

"At least I didn't just roll over for the first
woman who wanted to use my last name,"
Rush said.

Sam's temper sparked like dry kindling.
He carefully crumpled his sandwich wrap-
per into a tight ball of wax paper and foil. If
he gave voice to all the things on his mind,
their friendship would be nothing more than a
bloody lump on the deli floor and Rush would
be nursing a broken nose. "You've got your
methods. I've got mine," Sam said with de-
ceptive calm.

He pushed back his chair and gathered
up his trash. "Thanks for taking care of the
client," he said for the benefit of the man who'd
walked in.

"Sam, I'm—"

"Honest," Sam cut him off. Hearing an apology right now would make the turmoil churning through him worse. He walked out of the
deli without a word. Yes, he was furious with
Rush, but also with himself.

He walked by the bus stop and caught the
cable car on the next block, just to clear his
head and think. Hopeful he'd lost the men from

the sedan, he let the cool breeze off the bay blow through some of the delusions Rush had so helpfully pointed out.

No, he didn't really expect Madison to stick around and play the happy housewife once they sorted out her current problem. Despite the records he'd wedged into the Nevada system, she wasn't really his wife and his attraction to her notwithstanding, he couldn't just keep her in that role because it was the easy answer to his awkward social life. That would be the worst abuse of a friendship.

Worse than breaking your friend's nose because he pushed the truth in your face.

His only consolation was that she didn't seem to have a steady romance in her life beyond him as her false husband. Again, he wondered why she'd choose the solitude that a fake marriage would impose over an active dating life. She was smart and beautiful and accomplished. Her choices were another layer in the puzzle he was naturally inclined to solve.

Maybe Rush was wrong and he *could* keep Madison in his life. Not because he was a coward, but because the solution could work for both of them. There were worse reasons to create a partnership and call it a marriage. They'd need to discuss it. He would show her the pros and cons and listen to her hopes and concerns. Then they could draw up a contract and—

The bump and pinch at his side yanked him out of his pleasant thoughts. "Phone and wallet," a man said in heavily accented English. "Give over now."

"No," Sam answered. He glanced down under his arm and saw the flash of a knife. The lousy timing was unbelievable. Did the mugger behind him not understand they were on a moving cable car? "Find another mark."

The knife sliced his shirt, nicked his skin. "I find you. Phone and wallet."

"All right. Take it easy." Sam knew the route, calculated the time to the stop and how the cable car would slow and brake. "Take that out of my side so I can move."

He couldn't get a good look at the man's face from this angle, though the mugger was close enough Sam could judge his general size. The mugger was shorter than Sam by an inch or two and that most likely gave Sam a reach advantage. Slowly reaching for his wallet, he let his elbow graze the man's torso. The guy felt lean, another advantage for Sam.

"This is my stop," Sam said as the cable car braked. "Let's finish this outside."

"Here and now," the mugger countered.

The people packed into the car shifted and swayed with the stop. Prepared to move, Sam sucked in a breath as the knife slid through his shirt and caught skin. Twisting, he drove his elbow into the mugger's midsection and followed through with a forearm to his throat. He gripped the mugger's collar and jumped off the cable car, bringing him along.

No one on the cable car or sidewalk appeared overly concerned about Sam or the mugger. Sam pushed the smaller man off the sidewalk and into an alley and slammed his knife hand against the hard stone of the building. The knife clattered to the ground and Sam kicked it away.

"Who are you working for?" he demanded.

The mugger tried to shake his head. "Me. Alone."

Sam made his opinion on that lie clear, with a quick punch. "Who?" he asked as the man wheezed. Sam gave him a shake, unconvinced this was a random robbery. The world didn't function under that much coincidence.

He catalogued the man's distinct Asian features, general height and build and guessed at the age. A full description was possible if he chose to report this. Going through proper channels would take time. "What do you want with me?"

"Wallet and phone." The man squeezed the words through Sam's tough grip. "Work alone."

Sam kept the man pinned to the wall with a forearm while he pulled out his phone and took a picture of him. "Last chance," he said. "Why me?"

The man shook his head. "Mistake."

"Fine." Sam kicked him just above his knee. The man slumped to the ground and Sam followed him down, keeping his voice low and controlled. "Tell whoever sent you they are swimming in the deep end now. Got it?"

The man nodded.

Sam snatched the man's knife and left the sorry excuse for a mugger groaning in the alley. By the time he'd doubled back and reached the Gray Box offices, the wound in his side burned as if he'd been stuck with a hot poker. He didn't think the mugger had gotten that much of him. His skin and shirt were sticky under his palm and the familiar copper-tinged scent of fresh blood stung his nostrils. Once he was safely inside the building, he moved straight to the men's room off the lobby to catch his breath and assess the damage.

He swore when he saw the shirt was beyond salvation. It had been a favorite. He stripped it away and dumped it in the sink for now. Swearing again at the gash in his side, he debated his options. The first aid kit wouldn't be enough. He needed stitches. And a clean shirt. If he went to the hospital, they'd insist on filing a report.

While the legalities didn't bother him, he had other things to get done first. He sent a text message and a picture of the wound to the gym where he boxed and added a request for a clean shirt. The trainers there had plenty of experience stitching up split eyebrows, ears and cheeks. A slice over his ribs wouldn't be any challenge for them.

He flushed the wound with warm water and soap while he waited for the reply. When it came, along with criticism about leaving his weak side open, Sam laughed at his reflection. In the context of the last twenty-four hours, he had to admit life had become infinitely more exciting.

Chapter Seven

5:45 p.m.

The girls' day Lucy had arranged had turned into one of the best days in Madison's recent memory. The massage therapist, a man with a body and face worthy of a Nordic god, had worked out the kinks and knots in her shoulders and neck. Thoroughly loosened up, she'd enjoyed at least a gallon of lime-ginger water provided by the caterer. Lunch had been the ultimate girl feast of salads, white wine, more water and delightful, purely feminine conversation.

Facials had followed lunch and Madison and Lucy indulged in mani-pedis while a private shopper turned the living room into an exclusive boutique. With little encouragement from

Lucy, Madison splurged on a week's worth of clothing covering everything from lingerie to a strappy, sexy little black dress. At least she had the shoes at Sam's condo to go with that one. The shopper had her sizes and notes about her style preferences and left Madison with a business card and instructions to call if she needed anything.

If this was life as Sam's wife, she could get used to it all too easily. While that love-struck teenager she'd been did a victory cheer at the idea, older and wiser Madison recognized the gross mistake of enjoying this level of service and indulgence. Though she'd paid for everything, guilt niggled at the back of her mind with each step she took deeper into this farce.

It was one thing to wear a ring and pretend to be married to a busy entrepreneur who never needed to be present in her career, much less her life. Now everyone knew her husband's name and *face* and she'd dumped him smack in the middle of her problems.

As she and Lucy lounged outside on the balcony overlooking the city marina and the Golden Gate Bridge, Madison asked again how Lucy had pulled this off.

"Connections," Lucy said. "The people you

met today I met through my MBA grad work. Having a secret password known as Rush Grayson doesn't hurt."

Madison sipped her wine and circled a foot, admiring the bright berry polish on her toes and the perfect daisy decorating her big toe.

"I heartily approve of your whimsical side," Lucy observed with a smile. "Sam needs that in his life."

Madison was too relaxed to start protesting again. Besides, it was probably true about Sam. Lucy would know. "I could use it too," she replied.

"You finally look as relaxed as you should." Lucy tapped her wineglass gently to Madison's. "Cheers, my friend."

Madison wanted Lucy to be a friend. She, like Sam, often pushed everything other than work to the edges of her life. "I am relaxed, although I spent too much of the day imagining Special Agent Spalding storming the gates."

"All the more reason to enjoy a girls-only safe space," Lucy said.

Madison swirled the wine in her glass. "Have you heard from Rush?"

"Not since he messaged me about installing the new cyber security update at the museum."

Lucy sighed. "We'll have to tell them the dinner plan soon or they'll insist on having pizza at the office."

"Is that typical?"

"Less often since Christmastime," Lucy said with a wink. "I call myself the good influence. Melva, the woman who has kept that pair straight since the start, helps me get both Rush and Sam out of the building as often as possible."

"I bet Sam is tough to budge."

"You do know him well," Lucy observed, her gaze on the sun-warmed water.

Well seemed like an overstatement. Madison simply made educated guesses based on how he'd behaved in the past and what she read in the tech and business journals. "I'd be happy to cook for the four of us," Madison offered, shifting the topic to safer ground.

"With that manicure? Absolutely not. I made reservations already."

"Out?" A double date sounded like the perfect cap for her day. Except, marriage rumors aside, she wasn't actually dating Sam and doing something so public went against the orders from the legal department. All Sam needed was for his name and face to get dragged through the gossip columns again as his wife got yanked away from dinner by the FBI.

"I can hear the wheels turning in your head, Madison." Lucy tipped down her sunglasses. "If the FBI or any other agency had issued a warrant, we'd know about it. If your boss tried to reach you on your cell or email, Sam would've told you. We'll take your new dress on a test drive with a lovely dinner at a private dining room. Then you can test out that new lingerie for dessert," she finished with a grin.

"The shoes that go with that dress are at Sam's," Madison said.

"He can bring them along when they pick us up."

Madison gave in with a weary chuckle. "You really are a force of nature."

"I confess I've always been headstrong." Lucy gave her long, dark hair a sassy flip over her shoulder. "What's the point of knowing what you want if you don't go after it?" She sighed, thoroughly content. "There was a point when I thought I'd settle," she mused. "I'm glad I didn't and more important, I'm glad I took the second chance when it rolled around."

Madison thought about that as it related to

her desire for Sam and nearly choked on her wine. Going "after" Sam was likely to get her tossed out on her ear—a consequence she wasn't prepared to face.

Lucy's phone rang with an incoming call rather than the text message chime. She frowned at the screen and excused herself to answer.

Madison wasn't entirely comfortable out here alone with her thoughts. Every stately black sedan or beefed-up SUV left her feeling vulnerable and exposed. The daisy on her toe lost its whimsy as she beat herself up for slacking off instead of working to sort this out. Her boss said lie low. Extreme pampering and private power shopping didn't seem to fit with that order. Something was very wrong and she'd been out of touch for an entire day. No news cycle, no staff meeting, no assessment and discussion of last night. Without Lucy out here distracting her, Madison's contentment fizzled.

What had Spalding been looking for in her apartment? She didn't have anything to hide, but she knew things could get twisted around and misinterpreted during an investigation. What did he think he'd found?

As the tension gripped her shoulders, threatening to undo the benefits of the massage, she set her wine aside and tried to meditate. She hadn't made it halfway through the first round of breathing before Lucy returned.

"We're still on for dinner," Lucy declared brightly. "Rush is sending a driver to pick us up. He and Sam will meet us at the restaurant. I told Sam to bring the shoes," she finished with a brilliant smile.

Too brilliant, Madison realized. "What's wrong?" She got to her feet.

A quick debate played out over Lucy's expressive face. "Rush said they wanted to wait until after dinner to discuss it," she said.

"Discuss what?"

"Everyone is okay, I promise. The guys don't want to ruin dinner."

Madison folded her arms over her chest and waited. Lucy wasn't the only woman who could be a force of nature when necessary.

Lucy huffed out a breath. "Fine. In your shoes I'd insist on knowing too." She drew Madison back down to sit on the chaise beside her. "Someone tried to mug Sam this afternoon. Don't worry, he's completely fine! I made Rush put him on so I could talk to him myself."

Madison sucked in a breath. "What happened? I thought they'd be together."

"The important thing to remember is the mugger wasn't successful." She rubbed Madison's clenched fists. "Relax. Rush tells me Sam handled himself."

"Did Sam get a description?"

"Better," Lucy said. "He took the mugger's picture. Rush has one of his investigators working on the identification as well as pulling any prints or DNA from the knife."

The wince on Lucy's face when she realized what she'd said would've been comical under better circumstances. "I want to talk to Sam," Madison said.

"He's fine, I promise. He asked me to assure you he'll tell you everything tonight."

Madison looked around for her cell phone out of habit and swore when she remembered why it had been such a quiet, peaceful day. "I can't stand being out of the loop this way. I don't think I'm wired for hours and hours of bliss."

"Of course you are," Lucy soothed. "It just takes some practice." She checked the time on her phone. "Let's go ahead and dress for dinner. You'll feel better when you see Sam hale and whole."

Madison tried to get into the spirit of it as she and Lucy dressed and fussed with makeup and hair until the last possible second. They chatted over the silly look of Madison in the black dress and flip-flops on the short drive to a restaurant a block past Ghirardelli Square.

Lucy was right. As the driver parked at the side entrance and Sam stepped up to the car looking perfectly healthy and stunning in a dove gray suit, his pale blue dress shirt open at the collar, a wave of relief crashed over Madison. He opened the door and Lucy slid out. Before Madison could follow, Sam motioned her back and joined her in the backseat.

"Have a great time," Lucy said to him, closing the door.

The car pulled away from the curb and Madison stared at Sam, hoping he'd explain. Although her evening shoes dangled from his fingers, he seemed to have forgotten them as he stared back at her. "You look great," he said.

The fascinated intensity in his deep brown eyes turned her muscles to jelly as effectively as the massage therapist. "Thanks," she replied. "I know you can't possibly want to be out on the town two nights in a row."

"I'm okay if it's just the two of us." He handed her the shoes. "I know how to talk with you."

The two of us had such a lovely ring to it and the sincerity in the statement melted something inside her as she slipped her feet into the heels, careful of the small burn on the top of her foot.

Sam finally broke eye contact and sank into the cushions. "I'm sorry for the cloak and dagger routine. It's been a long day. Did you have a good time with Lucy?"

"Yes," she replied. "Don't take this the wrong way, but you look a little less fine than Lucy implied."

Sam dropped his head back on the seat and pushed his glasses to his forehead. With one hand pinching the bridge of his nose, his other hand found hers. "I'm not un-fine," he said after a long moment.

"Is that a word?" It was the only question she could think of with his hand wrapped around hers as if they sat this way every day. It felt more intimate than dancing last night. Despite the obvious toll of his day, this particular moment gave her an unexpected sense of contentment.

He turned his head and offered her a faint smile. "I sure as hell hope so."

She smiled back. "What can I do for *you*, Sam?"

His brown eyes glinted and his mouth opened before he abruptly changed his mind and snapped it shut again. "Just enjoy yourself tonight," he said after a long moment.

She wondered what he left unsaid. With all her practice reading people, interpreting the signs behind the words, Sam remained a mystery. "I will. I already am enjoying myself," she replied. It was a simple truth and if she wanted him to open up, she figured she should set the example.

"Lucy knows how to pack the most fun into an impromptu girls' day," she began. "I almost forgot why we were doing it in the first place."

"Lucy probably had that plan in motion before they reached the condo," Sam said. "It just made selling it to you easier when your boss asked you to stay out of the office."

"I understand the necessity for that." Madison let her gaze roam over the passing city. "It shouldn't have been a surprise that I'm uncomfortable being out of touch. Have you heard anything more about the FBI search of my apartment?"

"Heard or gone snooping?" he asked.

She faced him, hoping he had news. "Either."

"I'm good enough to do the snooping," Sam said, a wicked grin flashing across his face, "but I promised not to hack the FBI again for a year."

She gawked at the comment, realized he was serious and burst into laughter. "Does Special Agent Spalding know about your promise?" she asked when she caught her breath.

"Probably." He sat up straight in the seat and righted his glasses. "Never met him before last night," he added.

It was clear his mind was moving through scenarios and options invisible to her. He had a remarkable ability to pay attention to his surroundings without appearing to care or listen. It was an ability that made the experience all the more intense when he focused completely on her.

She wasn't entirely surprised or pleased to learn neither age nor determination dimmed her feminine reaction to him. Not even the circumstance—her *lie*—that had shoved them together. She was starting to think being older only made her reactions worse.

She swallowed. "What are you thinking?" she asked, certain the answer wouldn't be what she wanted to hear.

"I'm thinking about you," he said.

Madison drew in a small breath, caught in a web she'd created where delight and caution tugged her in opposite directions. Sam wasn't a flirt and he'd never looked at her as more than a friend. "What are you thinking about me?" She tried to regret the breathy way the words emerged, but when his gaze landed on her lips, she couldn't manage it.

Did he—could he—feel this electric chemistry in the air? She desperately hoped it wasn't all one-sided.

"Well, you and your apartment," he amended.

She knew better than to let her hopes about Sam take flight. She had to find a way to control this unquenchable crush. "I see."

He reached up and wrapped his finger around one of the curls framing her face. "Your hair is softer tonight."

"Thank you?" Startled he'd noticed, she wasn't sure how to take that compliment. Considering the source, she forced herself to accept that the words might be a polite, straightforward observation.

"Last night, pulled back, it was sleek and cool. Unapproachable." He frowned, his thoughts carrying him away momentarily. "Tonight you look warmer. More like yourself."

She was starting to feel downright hot, her body overheating from the supreme effort of staying still when she wanted to launch herself at him. She smiled in reply, not trusting her voice.

The car glided to a stop and Sam covered her hand with his. "You're not afraid of boats, are you? I should've asked earlier."

"No." She didn't remind him they lived in a city surrounded by water.

His face lit up in a big smile. "Good."

He offered his hand as she climbed out of the car and she stared at the luxury sailboats, cabin cruisers and yachts docked around the marina. She caught Sam's low voice, but not the words, as he gave instructions to the driver. "Let's go," he said, taking her hand in his again.

They didn't chat along the way. The evening was calm and yet curiosity and anticipation danced over her skin. What did he have in mind? She worked to remind herself they were friends only. He was here to help her through a temporary crisis.

"Here we are," he said, stopping at a narrow gangway at the end of the dock.

"You said boat." She'd expected a cruiser and Sam had brought her to a yacht. It was a large, well-appointed vessel with a crew of five standing by ready to welcome them aboard. "Is this yours?" she whispered as they followed the steward into a plush salon with a dinner table set for two.

"Rush owns it," Sam replied. "He uses it primarily to wow potential clients and shares it with the executive staff."

"*Wow* is right."

Another uniformed man asked for their drink preferences. Sam ordered a beer and she requested water, knowing another drink on an empty stomach would only make it harder to keep her hands to herself. The vessel glided away from the dock and they settled into soft chairs on the stern deck. The water churning in their wake as the vessel quietly moved into the bay mesmerized her. "Why didn't he and Lucy come along tonight?"

Sam studied the bottle of beer in his hand for a long moment. "A few reasons."

She waited, sensing his shift to practical issues. Whatever intimacy she'd imagined was blowing away in the sea air.

"After everything that happened today," he continued, "we adjusted the arrangements tonight so you and I could speak privately with no worry about interruptions."

"Does 'everything' include you being mugged?"

"Everything includes an *attempted* mugging," he clarified with a smile.

She noticed the smile didn't put a spark in his brown eyes. "You're not okay."

"I am." He shifted in the chair. "I got the man's picture and his knife." He sipped the beer. "The guy got nothing from me."

Madison wasn't so sure about that. Something serious weighed on his mind, had him more distracted than usual. "Will you tell me the whole story?"

"Maybe later." He sat back in the chair and propped an ankle on his opposite knee. "First of all, the museum and the white jade cup are now secure from online threats through the run of the exhibit. Rush just finished installing the new program as a courtesy trial. If they want to keep it when the exhibit returns to China, they can buy it."

"That was more than generous," she said. He had her almost convinced he was simply a carefree, wealthy entrepreneur out for a private dinner cruise. She spotted the tension in his clean-shaven jaw and the uncharacteristic stillness of his hands.

"You didn't want us to give them the upgrade for free?" He shot her a quizzical look.

"Why would I want that?"

"I just thought as a friend or whatever we are here, you might expect us to throw in a freebie."

"Sam, that's ridiculous." Too edgy and overwhelmed from the events of the previous twenty-four hours, she couldn't hide her offense. "Stopping the hacker pro bono was all the favor I needed. You're brilliant and should be paid well for your expertise." On a roll now, she ignored the curious lift of his dark eyebrows. "I'm well aware how much you and Rush give back to the community. You have every right to call me on the marriage lie and yet here we are, acting it out."

"Right down to our first fight, apparently," he said.

The charming grin made her knees weak. "You know what I mean."

He nodded, his gaze full of an earnest sincerity. "I'm happy to help you, Madison. We've been friends a long time."

She didn't trust herself to reply.

"I've been through your computer." He stayed her protest with a raised palm. "Off network. No one will ever know it was even turned on. I needed to study and evaluate your typical habits on that computer."

Work computer, she reminded herself. Her personal documents and such were in a password-locked file on her tablet at home. Great. Spalding probably had that now. Not that there was anything more incriminating than her banking and charity interests. Unless she counted every saved email she'd ever received from Sam Bellemere along with an electronic scrapbook of headlines he'd made through the years. If anyone found that, her fake husband might have cause for a restraining order against her.

"Madison, you're not listening. I know the details can be tedious—"

"It's not the details," she said quickly. "You've always made the details interesting for me." Through necessity, she'd developed the ability to listen to and assess multiple topics simultaneously. "The computer behavior assessment algorithms to prevent hacking and breaches are cutting edge."

"Yes, they are."

She sat forward, eager to hear more about what he was developing and what he'd do with it. "Will Gray Box market the new software publicly?"

He frowned at her. "You were listening."

She smiled and sipped her water.

"We're a long way from having a reliable program ready to market." He tipped his head back as they passed under the Golden Gate Bridge. "What's more important and relevant is the string of recent email messages I found buried in your official inbox."

She shivered and it had nothing to do with the chilly breeze on the bay. Sam set aside his beer and removed his suit jacket, sliding it over her shoulders. Being surrounded by the fabric warm from his body and the scent of his cologne was almost better than dancing with him at the gala. He lingered there in front of her fussing with the jacket panels as if he didn't want to go back to his own seat.

If she leaned forward just a few inches, she could kiss those firm lips and learn the taste of him at last. He was right there, within easy reach and she lost her nerve, too afraid of scaring him off. Far more frightened that kissing him would snap that last thread of hope that she might be content with another man.

"I clean out my inbox every day," she said, though the words came out as if she'd been chewing sandpaper. "I have folders and a system and—"

"I know." He pushed back from her. Standing, he tucked his hands into his pockets. "Behavior, remember?"

"Then where and how did I miss these emails you found?"

"It's not easy to explain. The dates and times show up over the past three or four months, but they didn't actually hit your inbox until after the gala. More specifically, just after the first disturbance call from your neighbors."

The inexplicable and sudden rash of trouble bumped around in her head until it fell into place. "You believe I'm being set up."

"Yes," he replied, his gaze searching the night beyond their boat. "I just can't pin down why."

Her mind raced back through recent months and the attempts on the State Department firewall. "What did the emails suggest?"

He sighed. "The implication is an ongoing conversation that you're interested in sharing confidential information about Vietnam's interests with China for the right price."

"I would never." She swore. "That's outrageous."

"I know."

"No wonder Spalding is after me. My boss said the FBI got a tip that I've already taken payoffs. It must be this hacker, or a group, trying to embarrass the State Department."

"I agree. Having more than one person or group come after you right now is too much of a coincidence. Unfortunately, it will take me some time to identify him." He removed his glasses and hooked them at the open collar of his shirt. "I've worked on this all day, Madison. Depending on how things come to light, the problems at the reception could be read as retaliation for your potential betrayal. That's a spitball theory, of course," he said quickly. "There are too many unknowns right now. Even looking at the pieces separately, it's clear to me the hacker has latched on to you. He or she took offense at your suddenly publicized marriage and me as your high-profile husband."

She understood why she might be a target as a liaison, but why did the appearance of a husband make any difference? She'd been behaving as married for a long time. "Should we publicize a separation or divorce instead?"

"Hell, no."

His swift reply had her looking up at him in shock. "What are you suggesting?"

"I can take care of myself." He picked up his beer and drained it. "You—we—have options. FBI involvement or not, Rush and I can get you out of the country. Tonight, if you like."

She glanced around the harbor as understanding of their location struck home. "You're suggesting we sail to Canada?"

"It's closer than Mexico," he quipped. "I'm just laying out your options," he added.

"Lay out another one. I'm not running from some punk hiding behind a wall of technology."

"Have you forgotten I used to be that punk?" he asked with a rough bark of laughter.

"Oh, you were not." She stood up, swaying a little with the movement of the boat as she walked over to the rail. She gripped it hard, willing herself to find a graceful way out of this twisted mess. "Lay out another option," she repeated over her shoulder.

"All right." He came up beside her and covered one of her chilled hands with his. "What if we enjoy what is sure to be an outstanding dinner and then head back to my place and handle whatever is coming together as husband and wife?"

She studied his profile, seeing none of the tension or stress in the hard square of his jaw, only resolute determination. "Together?" She was bewildered as much by the offer as she was by the easy way he delivered it.

"Exactly." He faced her, giving her a heated, toe-curling smile.

If only it would be that easy. "You stepping up publicly as my husband could very well put Gray Box at risk."

"I've factored that in."

His absolute fearlessness despite the unknowns made her want him more as a friend and an ally as well as on a personal level. She hadn't known it was possible to sink deeper into her infatuation with him.

"What did Rush say?"

His gaze slid over her shoulder, as if he could see the office from here. "We discussed every angle of the situation and while there's no foolproof plan right now, we know our options and basic tactics."

"You expect me to live with you at your condo?"

"Yes. The building is covered by the best security team in the business," he said, his eyes on her again. "It's all legal too, should the FBI believe a hacker's antics and claims over the proof we'll eventually provide to clear you."

"What about your real life, Sam?"

"You're as real as my life has ever been outside of the office," he replied. "Seriously, it's the best solution for you."

He started to say something else but the steward stepped out, announcing dinner. Sam laced his fingers with hers as they walked into the salon. "I did speak with my mom, since she's a society page junkie."

"Oh, no." Madison groaned. "She must think

I'm the worst for dragging you into my fib," she said as Sam pulled out her chair at the table.

"Not at all." He took his seat across from her and waited while wine was poured. "I told her the 'true story.'" He added air quotes to the phrase. "The way you gave it to me."

Appalled, Madison struggled to catch a full breath. "You didn't." His mother must be furious and hurt. "Sam."

"I admit she wasn't happy we eloped. She was thrilled to hear I have a wife who adores me."

Sheer embarrassment heated her cheeks. He'd figured out her infatuation. The stereotype that tech experts had no personal observation skills was thoroughly debunked. Sam, both a famous tech innovator and notoriously shy, a soft-spoken rejecter of typical social conventions, had recognized her desperate crush on him.

She knew it was all her fault. Yes, she could see his point about the need to play the parts she'd cast for them and the definite short-term benefits. What worried her more was the long-term fallout for her, him and the people who cared about them.

To her immense relief, any need for a response was delayed by the arrival of salads and a basket of aromatic herb bread, brushed with a gloss of melted butter. It gave her time to get a grip on her runaway thoughts so she could match his logical approach to this monstrously uncomfortable box she'd built.

Chapter Eight

"I explained our reasons," Sam continued, wondering about Madison's prolonged silence. Her cheeks were turning red, her lips caught tight between her teeth and she stared deliberately at her salad plate.

"You don't have to really adore me," he said quickly. "Obviously we won't be out and about much. I was selling it for Mom, that's all," he blathered on, fighting the rising panic. This wasn't how he'd envisioned the conversation. "I told her we kept the wedding quiet because it was better for your career not to go public until we had to."

"Had to," she echoed.

"Yes." He offered her a slice of bread and took one for himself. "To best protect you now, I think we'll need to let the public in a little more."

"My boss said lie low," she said. "Stay off the radar."

"I know." He leaned forward, willing her to look at him and see what he was offering. She didn't. "I promise you, Madison, we can manage this. We'll be careful and deliberate about the what, where and when of every piece."

"You'll hate that kind of invasion of your privacy."

He shook his head. As her husband, he wouldn't be coping with the scrutiny alone. It had been the personal teamwork he'd longed for. "We'll be invaded together." His joke fell flat. There had to be a way to convince her.

He'd spent all day thinking about it and decided this marriage offered them the best of both worlds. No longer an eligible bachelor, he could go out with his wife and enjoy the city without unflattering speculation or bizarre attempts to get his attention. Granted, when people approached him it was more often about technology than a personal interest in his life, but still. "Whatever attention we get, you can be a social asset for me. The company and I will be a legal buffer for you."

She met his gaze and her moss-green eyes were as cool and hard as the jade artwork in the exhibit. "You see that as an equal trade?"

He wished she'd spit out whatever was bothering her. Either his suggestion made her angry or there was more going on that she didn't want to share with him. "You're not enthused about this at all."

"My apologies." She raised her glass of wine. "A toast to wedded bliss." Her smile was brittle, far more fragile than the warm expressions they'd shared out on the deck.

He gently tapped his glass to hers and held her gaze as they sipped. "I've irritated you? Overstepped?"

"No." She closed her eyes a moment. "No," she repeated. "That's on me. I did the wrong thing with the guest list by dragging you into this on a personal level." She placed her hands in her lap, her body so still, her eyes solemn. "I appreciate the remarkable patience you've extended to me."

"There's more," he prompted when she picked up her fork and stabbed at the mixed greens on her salad plate. "I'd rather we were honest with each other." To that end, he should probably come clean with her about what he really wanted.

She choked, sputtered and then waved off assistance as both Sam and the steward moved to help her. "I'm okay. Maybe you should send me out of the country," she said morosely when the coughing spell was over.

Sam knew he didn't understand women, but this moodiness didn't fit with the Madison who'd shown exceptional grace under fire six months ago, last night and again this morning. When the salad plates were removed he walked over and pulled up a chair to her side of the table.

"Madison, I don't believe you're guilty of any wrongdoing."

"That's not it." She fanned her face with her hand and blinked rapidly.

He thought he caught the glimmer of tears welling in her eyes. He was bad enough at the personal stuff and lousy at soothing crying women. "If there's someone else in your life, I'll talk with him. I'll take care of the fake divorce as soon as this mess is resolved." Rush would have a field day that he couldn't keep a fake wife.

"No. There's no one else." She sniffled through a wry chuckle. "Only you."

"Same goes," he said, clutching her admission like a lifeline. Lasting marriages had started on weaker foundations. If he handled this crisis well, he might convince her to stay with him. Just because the situation was unconventional didn't mean it couldn't work. The more time he spent with her, the more he believed *they* could work.

"Pardon me?" Her eyes went wide, the soft green shimmering with emotions he couldn't label.

He understood that. He'd struggled all day with the potential pitfalls and, frustrated, he shifted his focus to the more enticing potential rewards. "Why don't we move forward with this?" He picked up her hand and kissed her knuckles, hoping she found the gesture romantic.

"This?" Her gaze locked on the point where his lips met her skin.

Probably laying it on too thick, he decided. Releasing her hand, he moved back to his side of the table as the main course arrived. "This," he said when they were alone. He pointed a finger between them. "Us. Being husband and wife. We'll play it out publicly, cautiously as your situation requires and in private we can see how we get along. I've drawn up a contract for your review with a plan to reassess and make adjustments in thirty days."

"What?" Her voice traveled up a full octave in the single syllable.

From the corner of his eye, he saw the steward hesitate before stepping out of view. Good. He didn't need witnesses to his humiliation. Sam sliced into the beef medallions and took a bite, savoring the flavor. He'd rather hear the litany of his inadequacies on a full stomach. Across the table Madison stared at him, still clearly mortified by his suggestion.

"I need you to clarify what you mean," she said with more edge than his steak knife. "Precisely."

"I am—" He caught himself before he used the word *propose* and started over. "In the simplest terms I am suggesting you move in with me for a month, with an option to extend our arrangement after that time."

"You think it will take that long to track down the hacker who is targeting me?"

"I can't be sure," he admitted. "For your career, I hope it won't take that long." He'd done his best to bait the jerk tampering with her email and State Department systems. "I can't make any promises on the timeline. The contract specifies that we live together for a month, regardless of any outside circumstances and see how being married works for us."

"You're serious." Her eyes went wide.

He gave her a smile, though it didn't ease the misery straining her lovely features. "It was your idea," he said kindly. "I'm taking it a step further, that's all."

Her knuckles turned white as she clutched her knife. "It was my cover. It wasn't meant to be real, Sam." She lowered her gaze. "I don't think I can pretend for thirty days," she finished on a whisper.

"Right." Of course she couldn't. She hadn't meant to pretend at all. She hadn't shared his name until she needed his skills, not him personally. Rush was right, he was a coward. A coward and an idiot for thinking he might win her over if only they spent more time together. A normal man wouldn't latch on to a convenient, familiar woman and try to shape a friendship into something more.

Seizing an unexpected opportunity was smart business. That didn't make it an equation for a workable personal interest. He was second-rate when it came to the small, attentive gestures women enjoyed, tonight being plenty of evidence of that. According to the advice from relationship experts he'd studied this afternoon while a few test programs cycled, women wanted men who could offer romance, consideration and responsiveness.

All things Sam didn't know how to give. He could save her career—probably—and keep her out of harm's way—again, probably—but it wouldn't be enough to give her a happy, fulfilled life. He didn't seem built for that. Even the women he'd dated, the ones after his money or financial backing on a business deal, didn't put up with him for long.

"You're right. I'm out of line. Forget I mentioned it. It wasn't meant to be this awkward. You take the condo and I'll stay at the Gray Box office until we figure out who's gunning for you. I respect our friendship, all evidence to the contrary. Use the condo," he repeated. "Use the marriage cover as long as you need it. You'll have all the legal resources Rush and I can muster until we clear your name. Whatever you need, personally or publicly, let me know and I'll be there."

Embarrassed and discouraged, he couldn't sit here and act as if nothing had happened. Knowing it was rude, he excused himself.

"Sam, wait."

"I'll be right back," he promised without turning around. Hell, he couldn't figure out why he was upset. It had been a long shot, trying to squeeze something more permanent out of a friendship. With luck, she'd forgive him by Christmas and he'd get another email card from her to add to the collection he'd saved through the years.

What the hell had he been thinking to take advantage of her on the basis of proximity when things were going to hell in her world? He might have talked with Rush about it. Better if he'd gone over his idea with Lucy for some female perspective.

"Sam!"

He kept walking, taking the stairs two at a time up to the upper level and out onto the open deck at the bow. He dragged in a deep breath and pushed his hands through his hair. The move made the fresh stitches in his side sting. Whose bright idea had it been to have this conversation on a damn boat where he couldn't get away from her? Rush's idea, he remembered. Though he hadn't confided his thirty-day plan to Rush, his best friend knew he liked to hole up with his computers when things got sticky. *Sticky* was definitely a nice word for the hole he'd dug for himself tonight.

"Sam, I'm sorry." Her hand landed on his shoulder, soft and gentle.

He held still, reveling in her touch despite his foolish behavior. "Don't apologize. This is on me. I made an outrageous suggestion," he said, unable to look at her.

Her hand smoothed down his arm, stopping just below his elbow. His entire body seemed to start at that particular point, all of his attention zeroed in on the feel of her.

"I'm grateful for all your help," she said.

"But?" He met her gaze, her eyes unfathomable in the starlight.

"No *but*s," she replied quietly.

She seemed to lean into him and he knew it had to be his imagination. Or the motion of the ship. Not of her free will. He didn't draw women in; he was the guy who ignored them until they drifted away.

"Do you remember the first day we met?" she asked.

She'd been wearing faded jeans with a tear

at one knee and a pink football jersey with the quarterback's number from the prior school year's powder-puff game. She'd moved with a ballerina's grace, making him feel more awkward than usual that day. "Vaguely."

"I asked if you could help me and you said you had to try."

"That sounds like me." Blunt and braced for rejection. "You were a good student."

"Thanks to you, my grades eventually reflected that." She shifted again, rubbing her hands over her arms. She was chilled again, having left his jacket in the salon. Even he knew giving her his shirt would be going too far.

"You should get out of the wind," he said.

"In a minute. I need to say this."

He waited, captivated now as she nibbled on her lip, her gaze sliding to his mouth, his chest, then away to the water. Whatever it was, she clearly wanted to keep it to herself. The polite thing was to let her off the hook. He was the poster child for privacy and yet he wanted to coax out all the mysteries lingering in her soft green eyes.

"I knew who you were when we were introduced," she said. "I knew why you'd been out of school the previous year."

He glanced away. "It wasn't a state secret."

"No. The secret was how much I admired you for taking the chance."

"It was a cocky stunt," he countered.

One narrow shoulder rose and fell. "You did something no one else had done. Plus…" She stopped, took a deep breath. "Plus I had the biggest crush on you."

He stared at her, waiting for the straight face to crack into laughter as she delivered the punch line. She didn't laugh, didn't add to the statement. "I don't get the joke." He shoved his hands into his pockets and leaned back against the rail.

"I'm not joking." She shivered a little and hugged herself tighter. "I had the biggest crush on you in high school and you were oblivious."

In his head he heard Rush teasing that Madison had liked him. "You dated…" His voice trailed off. He couldn't remember whom she'd dated, only that it hadn't been him. Of course, he'd never asked her out. She'd probably gone out with guys who had the confidence or bravado to speak to girls without stumbling over every other word. To call him a late bloomer was an enormous understatement for Sam's dating life.

"I didn't date," Madison said. "I went out with friends on the weekends."

"Strict parents?"

"Well, yes," she answered. "And the boy I really liked—you—was oblivious."

He could see her honesty in her eyes as easily as he could see the moon in the sky. "Madison, if you sent me signals back then, I'm sorry I missed them. Even if I'd noticed a signal, I was terminally shy and petrified of casual conversation." He reached out and rubbed her arms, chasing away the goose bumps. "My mom thought the tutoring would help me with the shyness and she convinced the judge to count it as my community service."

"Did it help?"

"Not really." He looked down into her gorgeous face with the sharp cheekbones, wide eyes and inviting lips. Out here in shadow and starlight, cruising across the inky velvet of the water, she looked delectable, a woman well out of his league. Still, he ached for her. She was smart to avoid one extra day of a fake marriage with him. His needs would overwhelm her and wreck their friendship within a week.

By the end of thirty days she'd be begging for the State Department to move her to New York or anywhere he wasn't.

"We should go inside," he repeated, forcing his hands away from the supple strength in her arms. "You're chilled."

She stepped closer, her legs bracketed by his, yet he was the one who felt trapped. He was caught in a sensual cage between her lithe body and the hard deck rail at his back. The ache ratcheted into a serious need. "Madison."

She lifted herself onto her toes, her body a soft glide against him and pressed her lips to his. An instant of featherlight contact and then gone.

The touch sent a frantic pulse skittering through him. Reaching out, he cupped her jaw in his hand, brushed her lower lip with his thumb. Her eyelids were heavy as he pushed his hand into her hair and brought her mouth back to his for another taste, a full taste. He kissed her, slowly at first, giving her room to push back or to tell him off. Instead, she sighed and the soft, wistful sound thundered in his ears. When her lips parted, he took the kiss deeper. Exploring the angles and touches that made her gasp and lean into him.

Desire and pleasure built touch by touch as the kiss deepened. Her palms were warm at his hips, her fingers digging in a bit for balance as the boat rocked. And then her hands slid up his rib cage, stirring bliss on one side and sparking fire on the other. He flinched at the pain.

She froze, eyes wide staring up at him. "What's wrong?"

"Nothing." He caught her before she could scramble away. "It's nothing." He was not losing this chance, not with that kiss rocking through him.

She ducked her head, evading his attempt to reclaim that stunning sensation. "Sam, look." She curled her fingers into her palms, then spread them wide and tugged at his shirt. "Wait, you're bleeding." With an accusing glare, she added, "You *are* hurt."

"I'm fine," he said while she pulled him toward the better light at the stairwell. "I'm sorry for bleeding on you."

"Oh, hush." She called for the steward and demanded hot water and towels. She supervised Sam's return to the salon and pushed him into a chair and started unbuttoning his shirt.

"This is escalating quickly," he observed. "I like it."

She rolled her eyes. "So says the man who offered me a thirty-day contract to cohabitate with an option to stay married."

"We all have our strengths." He wouldn't apologize. Not after that hot, searing kiss full of dark, tempting promises. He wanted more of her, all of her and preferably right now. Hackers, the FBI and diplomacy could wait in line for her attention. He wanted her, wanted to indulge his urge to spoil her with the best life could offer.

She tugged his shirt from his waistband and batted his hands out of the way when he tried to stop her. "I knew you looked pasty when you got into the car."

"Computer nerds always look pasty. It's the persistent lack of sunlight." His breath caught as she pressed a hot, damp towel to the stitches in his side.

"You have never been pasty," she countered. "Hold still."

He didn't have much time to appreciate what might have been a compliment. "I'm not sure that's supposed to get wet."

"It's not supposed to be bleeding either. Did the doctor give you any antiseptic ointment or instructions?"

"Are you a qualified nurse?" he asked, growing impatient. If she was going to put her hands on him, he had better suggestions for where to start.

"We have a doctor on board," the steward replied.

"Get him," Madison answered before Sam could reply. "This looks infected."

"It can't be. We cleaned it, stitched it up."

She pressed a dry towel to his side and covered it with his hand. "Easy pressure," she instructed. She used the warm soapy water and a second towel to wash her hands. "When you say 'we,' who do you mean?"

He stalled, hoping the doctor would distract her. She wasn't fooled.

"Sam." She took his chin and steered his face so he had to look at her.

Not that the view was any hardship. "You're prettier than ever," he said, hoping to distract her. She'd had a crush on him once and he didn't think she could kiss him that way if she didn't still like him a little. That hadn't been a kiss between friends.

"And you're going to answer me. Who put in these stitches?"

"One of the trainers from the gym." At her

obvious disgust, he quickly defended his choice. "I couldn't run out to a hospital without raising questions and causing more trouble."

"You might have been killed."

"This was more accident than intention," he said. She glared again. "I handled it." His pride bruised, he said, "I'm not the scrawny nerd I used to be."

Her eyes swept over his chest, exposed by the open shirt. "I noticed."

Was that a little flutter he heard in her voice, or was she simply exasperated and done with him? "Does that mean you approve of how I turned out?"

"I'd be either a fool or blind not to," she muttered, turning away. "Where is the doctor?"

He dropped the towel and caught up with her. "Maybe he fell overboard," he said, pressing his lips to the top of her shoulder. "This isn't serious."

"You were stabbed because of me."

"I was scratched, deeply," he agreed, turning her to face him. He couldn't figure out how to hug her without bleeding on her again. "The investigator is still working out if the incident had anything to do with the trouble surrounding your work."

"However you came by the injury, you've popped stitches and need them repaired." She stepped out of his reach as the doctor entered the salon.

Sam obediently stretched out on his back on a sofa and let the doctor come to his own conclusions.

"Not bad work," he said, prodding at the repair. "Just in a bad place. You need to take it easy for several days."

"Good thing nerd work isn't taxing," Sam replied, his eyes on Madison.

She snorted. He caught her staring at his chest again and wondered if they were finally thinking similar thoughts.

By the time the doctor finished, leaving him with another admonishment to rest, the steward had found a clean shirt for Sam. When he offered to serve fresh meals, Madison declined and Sam followed suit.

"Back to the city is best," Sam said.

Madison picked up her wine and stood at the window overlooking the stern deck. Sam joined her, keeping his silence. He didn't want to say the wrong thing and ruin any chance of kissing her again.

"I'm not signing any contract," she said at

last. "We don't need that kind of formality to do what's necessary."

"Okay." A string of what-ifs trailed through his mind, but he recognized that was his business sense clamoring for certainties that a personal relationship never demanded or guaranteed. "I'll follow your lead." That would be the best solution for both of them, publicly and privately. "Whatever you need, Madison, just ask."

Once they were back on land, he'd be preoccupied again with tracing the hacker and the tech issues. He wouldn't have the time or inclination to research how to romance and woo her the way she deserved. He would leave the next step, together or apart, up to her.

She lifted her face, those green eyes studying him. "What do *you* need, Sam?"

More time with you in my arms. He bit back the revealing response, annoyed with his infatuation and searched for a more palatable reply. "I need time to root out the hacker," he managed. "I believe I can do that and still play the role of your husband effectively." Good grief, could he make it sound more sterile or calculated?

"All right." She closed her eyes on him, on

the view and rubbed her temples. "While you work on the technical side, I'll keep prodding at the diplomatic side."

"Your boss told you to back off."

She snapped her eyes open once more. "He told me to take a honeymoon too. You'll need my expertise to find the hacker," she insisted. "The cause and motives he presented in the chat room before the museum stunt are bogus. If he's the same person or group accusing me of taking bribes, it's even more essential to know the nuances and intentions of all the parties involved."

Sam mulled that over as he considered the circumstances that had drawn him into her life again. "Reviewing what we have so far, I think he's after more than making his reputation with a notorious hack or new virus."

"I agree," she said.

"So we'll stick with the marriage cover story and stay off the radar together?" he asked, wanting to be clear about where they stood.

"At least until the FBI dumps me in a holding cell."

"That will never happen," he vowed.

She shook her head and more of her silky hair spilled out of the clip holding it, loosened by his hands and the breeze. "You say that now, but mine wouldn't be the first diplomatic career ruined by false allegations."

"You have me on your side," he said, wishing she'd accept everything he could offer. "And I have resources most people can't imagine." He wouldn't hesitate to employ any of them if it meant keeping a friend safe, keeping *her* safe.

As another tiny frown tugged at her lush mouth, he wondered why every reassurance he offered seemed to make her more uncomfortable. He told himself it wasn't relevant to the problem. Better to believe that than admit he still didn't have the guts to ask her out on a proper date.

Chapter Nine

They didn't speak at all on the drive from the marina to his building. Madison was grateful for the quiet. She needed time to think and to come to terms with the realization that he'd given his mother Madison's version of the truth. What did that mean? She had no idea. Just when she was sure she thought she understood this thing between them, he said something that made her doubt her conclusion.

At least by her refusing to sign the strange marriage test-drive contract, they seemed to be back on the stable footing of a friendship. After the doctor's visit, Sam had swiftly shifted back to business mode while she struggled to quell the pent-up desire thrumming through her veins. How was she supposed to feel about that?

He didn't touch her, aside from offering his hand to help her in and out of the car. She couldn't make up her mind if that fell into the pro or con category of the evening. Doctor's orders or not, having kissed him once, she wanted more. More kisses, more of that sensual way his hand in her hair made her body pliant. What would it be like to uncover his body inch by inch and explore the strength and shape of him? To learn what made him weak with desire? If they kissed again—preferably *when*—she would refuse to stop until she knew all of him and he'd learned all of her.

I'll follow your lead, he'd said. If he knew the images those four words evoked, he'd run away or drag her to the nearest bedroom and lock the door.

Although his "unimaginable resources" had been unquestionably helpful in her current crisis, she wanted to know Sam as a person, not as a wallet. The way he poked and prodded at any sort of problem or puzzle until he untangled the solution had always intrigued her. She might have had a crush on him, but that teenage fascination was shifting into something else with every passing hour. It sounded crazy in her head, standing next to one of the wealthiest, sexiest men in the world, to say she loved his mind first.

Loved?

She sighed, abruptly recognizing how much danger her heart was in. For a teenager, the concept of love came with loopy hearts and flower doodles. The real thing had been too big to even entertain. Growing up, being out in the world, she found it impossible to label her persistent hang-up on the cute, nerdy guy from high school as *love*.

In the elevator, she peeked at him from under her lashes. She wasn't feeling anything that qualified as cute or nerdy when she looked at him tonight. When they entered his condo, Sam said her name and her body pulsed with anticipation.

"I'm going to change clothes and get to work," he said.

The memory of his sculpted chest flashed through her mind. She bit her lip so she didn't beg him to let her watch.

Sam gave her an odd look. "If you're tired, you don't have to join me. We can pick up this discussion again in the morning."

"It's not that," she said breezily. Stepping out of her heels, she hooked the straps over her finger. "I'm thinking about the clothes." It was mostly true. "Lucy's private boutique today does me no good if my purchases are all at her place."

"It should all be here by now." He raised his chin toward her side of the condo. "I asked her to have everything delivered to your room." He turned in the opposite direction, heading for his office.

Excited to verify the claim, she hurried to the guest room. Her room, to use Sam's phrase, for the foreseeable future. While it was far better than a holding cell, living with Sam would give her plenty of other pitfalls to avoid. She couldn't believe she'd told him about crushing on him in high school or that she'd kissed him. She touched her fingers to her lips, recalling the feel of that amazing kiss. Oh, the risk had been worth it when he took control.

Desire warmed her skin and that quiver in her belly was back with a vengeance. She sank down on the bed, wondering if he'd meant it. Would he really follow her lead if she asked him to make love to her?

No, that was insanity waiting to happen. She didn't know how long they'd be stuck in this limbo. Immersion in Sam's daily life, without the distraction of her career, wouldn't be a dream come true. It would be a nightmare when the idyllic time ended. She had no illusions about his dedication to his work or his view of her as a friend. Just because a man knew how to leave her breathless with a kiss didn't mean he could love her. She'd been on the opposite side of the equation with a man who'd loved her in ways she couldn't return.

Because her heart was devoted to Sam.

She was an idiot, convincing herself her career would be enough satisfaction. That eventually the right man would walk into her life, a man she could trust with her marriage secret, a man who'd be patient while she undid that secret to make room for him. A man with qualities that would shatter everything she'd idealized about Sam.

Now that she'd kissed Sam, the man she'd fantasized about for nearly half her life, she knew her "someday" man didn't exist. It wasn't a pretty thought, being so enamored and infatuated and—yes, damn it—in *love* with a man who wasn't looking for the same thing from her.

A thirty-day test-drive marriage contract wasn't a marriage. Not the way she wanted to be married and share her life with someone. She didn't want to be his social butterfly. She wanted him to be more than a legal buffer for her. She wanted them. Together, as a team. Despite the sizzling potential packed into that kiss, she wanted a lifetime partnership with more lasting affection than sexual chemistry keeping them in the same room. She wanted them to be more to each other than various convenient reasons.

When she'd sought a psychologist to help her get over Sam as Mr. Perfect, she assumed they'd find an answer for her lingering crush. She'd anticipated that a professional could identify why she idealized him, that maybe he exemplified a particular quality or trait she admired.

No. The best suggestion to come out of a year working on the issue from every angle was that she should reach out to Sam and tell him her feelings. Accepted or rejected, that sort of action would allow her to move on. He'd been spotted around town that holiday season with a regular date, an actress he'd met while consulting on a movie project in Los Angeles. She'd sent the usual Christmas card and put a lid on her feelings.

Unfulfilled sexually and emotionally, she carried the lavender sleep set with her into the bathroom. Pulling the pins from her hair, she brushed it out, then piled it high on her head, securing it with a band to keep it out of the way while she washed her face. She reached back to unzip her dress and felt the zipper catch in the fabric. Twisting around, fumbling with it, she couldn't quite wriggle out of the dress. On a heavy sigh, she accepted she had unpleasant choices. Ask Sam for help, cut the dress off or sleep in it and hope for a better result in the morning.

Embarrassed and frustrated, she stalked across the condo to his office and knocked on the open door.

"Come in." He sounded annoyed and for a second Madison reconsidered not disturbing him.

"I'm stuck," she said, stepping forward into his domain.

"Me too," he muttered without turning. He'd changed clothes. A black T-shirt stretched across his back and he'd pulled on gym shorts. His feet and legs were bare. The man did not get that body from his "nerd work" career in cyber security and development.

She dragged her gaze away from the delicious view of him to the monitors that held his attention. It wasn't code or museum protocols. Those were articles and reports about the situation and key players in the South China Sea. She came closer until she was able to read over his shoulder.

"Resources," she murmured. "You weren't kidding." He'd tapped into reports that were stored behind layers of security and permissions.

"I've gone back and forth through the instances where the museum hacker took credit. He shows up with an affiliation with a group of American radicals who claim we've sold out to China, but in the hacks, the code and language are just different enough to make me think that's bogus."

She was skimming articles on the other monitors. "This guy doesn't care about the fishing rights or shipping lanes in the South China Sea. It's only an excuse, something that matters to the countries I work with as a liaison."

Sam leaned back in his chair. "You do realize China and Vietnam will never be good friends."

"We just need them to be civil," she replied in her cool, State Department voice.

"I keep asking myself what anyone gains by embarrassing you or sending the FBI into your apartment."

"Distraction? Collateral damage?"

"No."

His stern reply pulled her attention and she glanced down to find him staring up at her as if she was one more piece of research he needed to solve the puzzle. Before her eyes could lock with his mouth, she forced her gaze back to the monitors. "These articles aren't related," she said, trying to stay on point.

"Why haven't you changed clothes?" he asked.

"The zipper is stuck," she said. "Hang on. You shouldn't have access to this report." She pointed to a draft of a report she'd written last year. The final version had supposedly been sent up the line and stored on secure State Department servers.

He followed her finger. "Technically, I don't have access."

"Sam." Fresh panic made her palms sweat. "My boss told me not to log on." They'd need to come up with an excuse and fast. She thought of calling the office, but it was late and Sam had her phone too.

The chair creaked. Sam stood up and walked around behind her. "Relax."

At his touch she jumped, having blanked on the real reason for entering his office.

"Madison, it's okay. You're not logged in. Neither one of us has disobeyed your boss." He pointed out a flat black rectangle. "That report was copied from your hard drive and the copy was made in my secure lab when I picked apart your laptop."

"Oh." She clamped her mouth shut when one of his hands slid between the fabric of her dress and her skin as he started working the zipper at her back. Finally it gave, lowering with a slow, subtle rasp to the base of her spine. The office air was cool as the panels parted, exposing her bare skin to his view and the warmer touch of his fingers.

"Thank you." Too late, she remembered the new black lace lingerie with the sexy red bow at the back that he could probably see perfectly. If she asked, would he put those lips to her skin?

"Do you still dance?" His rough voice set her pulse skipping.

"No." Her last performance had been for a stage production during the spring semester of her sophomore year of college. "I take ballet classes when I can, just to unwind. There's a studio near the office."

"You move so gracefully," he murmured. One blunt fingertip trailed down her spine to her bra strap and back to the nape of her neck.

How could there be so much pleasure, so much significance, in that small caress? She turned to face him, feeling exposed by far more than the open panels of her dress. She ached to wrap herself around him and caught herself as the doctor's orders clanged through her mind. Sam needed rest. The best way to be sure he obeyed that order was to stay up with him. "I'll be right back," she said.

Behind his glasses, he blinked a couple of times. "You don't have to stay up with me."

"I'm your best resource. That's fact, not ego," she assured him, pushing her lips into a smile. If she could focus on the puzzle the way he did, she'd get through this in one piece. "Give me just a minute."

She dashed back to her room and shimmied out of the dress. She pulled on her new denim shorts and a boxy loose-weave sweater, pushing up the sleeves to her elbows. When she returned to his office, he was back in his chair studying the multifaceted issues between the countries she served as liaison. He'd pulled up the second chair beside his.

"Why did China choose to feature the white jade cup?" he asked when she sat down.

"We've been working on this exhibit for more than a year. They want to show Americans a trusting, touchy-feely side to encourage understanding and foster cooperation."

"Did we send something to a museum over there?"

She chuckled. "People. In general our best-received asset overseas is our innovation." She explained a bit more about what the cooperative effort entailed.

"Tell me about Liu." Sam's hands were bringing up the general information from typical online searches of the name. "How long have you known him?"

She watched him work while she explained the developing professional relationship. Sitting here, talking over the issues with him, was so satisfying and compelling. "Why don't you like him?"

Sam shrugged those broad shoulders and then stretched his arms high overhead. "I don't dislike him. You know I'm better with computers than people."

She disagreed, though she kept the thought to herself.

"Some of the questions he asked at the reception made me uneasy."

That put Madison on alert. "What questions?"

Sam waved off her concern. "Rush and I can get paranoid when people ask about our software."

"He wanted to talk about Gray Box during the reception?"

"We have a global reach," Sam said. "He's probably a customer."

She stifled a yawn and checked the clock. They were creeping up on midnight and he seemed fresh as ever. She pulled her feet up to the chair and wrapped her hands around her knees. "That's not what you mean."

"No. I ran it by Rush. It might've been a polite way to show interest, the way you described him. Something about it felt like fishing, but what do I know?"

Quite a bit. She kept that thought quiet, as well. "He can't want to poach you," she said.

"His personal business interests don't run to software."

Sam didn't reply. He was rolling the mouse around another article until his gaze had landed on her toe. "How did I miss this?" He leaned over for a closer look at the daisy.

Her heart hammered. Being the object of his single-mindedness made her knees weak and her skin prickle with awareness. "Spur of the moment, girl day decision," she said in a voice barely more than a whisper. She wiggled her toe, silently inviting him to touch.

He did. That one teasing stroke along the tip of her toe had her biting back a moan. "It suits you." When he met her gaze the yearning in his brown eyes scorched her.

"I want to kiss you," she admitted.

"I'm right here," he replied. He swiveled a bit, tugged her chair closer to his between his knees. He ran his hands over her feet, up to her knees and back down.

"Sam, the doctor said—"

His lips twitched up at one corner. "He isn't here." He ran his hands up to her knees and down over her thighs this time, his fingertips sliding just under the hem of her shorts before retreating. Started over.

Feeling boneless, she was primed and ready for him already.

"Your legs are gorgeous," he said. "I could do this all night."

She'd never survive it if he didn't do more.

"Your lead," he reminded her.

Her pulse stuttered, but her hands were steady as she laid them over his on top of her knees while she caught her breath. She dropped her feet to the floor and leaned into him. Stroking the length of his arms, she relished the thick, carved shape of his biceps, the solid curves of his shoulders. She dragged her hands down the hard angles of his chest and teased the skin of his stomach just under the hem of his shirt.

She wet her lips, watched his eyes, dark with need, follow the motion.

Her lead. She eased her chair back, hiding a smirk when his eyebrows dipped into a frown. He would let her go, she knew it. She wanted to stay right here in this moment. With him. Standing, she peeled her sweater off over her head, let it fall to the floor. His frown was gone, his eyes on the black lace bra as he ripped off his T-shirt.

She laughed when he hooked a finger into

the waistband of her shorts and tugged her closer. Leaning down, she kissed him, with all the tenderness and urgency a lifetime of fantasies had built up. She poured all she had into those kisses, everything she wanted to share with him and didn't dare speak the words. His wide palms slid up her back and she pushed her fingers through his hair as he nuzzled her breasts through the lace. Then he flicked open the bra clasp and tossed the lingerie aside, his mouth closing over the tight peak of one nipple. She arched into the marvelous heat of his mouth. He nipped and suckled and tormented each breast in turn until he was her only balance.

"This is better than any fantasy," she whispered.

He chuckled, the light stubble on his chin rasping her sensitive flesh as his mouth blazed a trail down to her navel. "Just wait."

He dropped to his knees and popped open the button of her shorts, lowered the zipper. His tongue dipped and swirled over her skin, inch by inch as he dragged the denim shorts down her legs. He lifted her foot and planted a kiss on the toe sporting the daisy.

"Gorgeous legs," he said again. The words

hummed against her skin as he kissed a meandering path from her foot to her inner thigh.

She looked down into his hot brown eyes and surrendered the lead to him. He slipped a finger beneath the thin triangle of black lace and she gasped and bucked at the intimate touch. She was slick and ready, rolling her hips to meet each passionate caress. His devotion was clear in every velvety touch of his tongue, hot press of his lips and bold, claiming touch of his hands.

His name burst from her lips when she climaxed and he caught her, cradling her close when her knees threatened to buckle. "Hang on to me." He surged to his feet, carrying her into his bedroom.

"Your stitches."

"I can only feel you," he said.

Stretched out on his massive bed, she was mesmerized by his body as he stripped off his shorts. "You're a sculptor's dream." She sat up on her knees and he let her hands trace the fascinating ridges and hollows of his torso. She peeked at the injury—which looked fine now—and reached lower, her fingers circling his arousal. He closed his eyes and dropped his head back as she explored and experimented with what pleased him.

Groaning, he rolled her back and kissed her until they were both breathless. "What about your dream?" He trailed kisses over her ear, along her jaw, down the column of her throat. The dusting of hair on his chest teased her aching nipples.

His erection pulsed against her entrance in the sweetest torture. She opened her legs, wrapping them around his. Brushing his hair back from his face, she gave him the truth. "You've always been my dream, Sam."

Holding her gaze, he filled her with one full, deep thrust and her body gripped him in response. He pulled back, just a little and thrust again. She matched his driving rhythm, craving more and more. She clutched his arms as the pleasure built and the second climax ripped through her moments before he found his release.

Sated, she kissed him lazily as he relaxed and stretched out beside her. When he tucked her into the warm shelter of his body, it was such a remarkable sensation she stayed awake as long as possible to savor the experience.

Chapter Ten

Sam blinked awake, startled by the soft glow of sunlight creeping around the edges of his bedroom windows. He never slept past dawn. More startling, Madison's supple legs were twined with his. Careful not to disturb her, he reached for his watch. Just past seven. He couldn't recall the last time he'd slept for six hours straight.

"You're a wonder," he whispered, kissing her forehead. She challenged him, tempted him and seemed to genuinely care for *him*.

Regardless of the many ways she wowed him, he hadn't intended to leave his search for the hacker undone overnight. Slipping out of bed, he went to the bathroom to clean up and get back to work. The sooner they put her life back together, the sooner he could start working on his next challenge: convincing her to remain his wife.

While she slept, Sam picked up their scattered clothing and dumped it in his hamper before settling at his desk. He poked at the original code some more, testing theories and runs, making little progress. Nothing had popped on the traps he'd set to locate the hacker either. He was halfway through a second cup of coffee and still didn't have a rock-solid plan to keep Madison safe and restore her career. He wasn't convinced that preventing another attack on the exhibit would annoy the hacker enough to force a mistake. There was an element he was missing. He could sense it; he just couldn't pin it down.

Restless, Sam messaged the investigator Rush had assigned to the mugging incident. With a little luck, that would create a lead they could follow. Sam agreed with Madison that this hacker had an agenda beyond the crap he—or she—was spouting.

Her boss wanted her away from the office. The FBI had yet to demand an interview with her. Still, the pieces swirled around in his mind and he sensed a storm waiting for the perfect conditions to become a hurricane.

Sam fought the temptation to jet away and put her well and truly out of danger. He had the resources, rabbit holes both online and real-world, where they'd never be found. What the public *thought* they knew about him hardly qualified as the tip of the iceberg. Billionaire was a number—an amazing number that garnered immediate influence—but it didn't define him. Brilliant innovator meant more and fit him better, although people generally didn't want to understand how he worked his way from broad concept to finished product.

Madison deserved to hear equivalent praise from her peers. She'd worked hard to make her dreams a reality. Having seen her in action, he knew removing her from that would be akin to taking away his computers and access. Those months in juvenile detention had been the worst of his life. He couldn't do that to her, wouldn't cut something so vital from her life.

I admired you, she'd said. The recollection was nearly as shocking as hearing her say those words last night. No one said things like that to him and never for getting caught in a criminal act.

He had definitely been oblivious of any admiration she'd expressed when they were kids. Of course he'd been wearing the angst and piss-poor attitude as a badge of honor with the singular tenacity unique to teenagers. By some miracle and no small credit to his mom, he'd churned that angst into drive and focus and here he was, on top of the world and so lonely that he'd offered his friend a contract to stick around.

She should've pushed him overboard rather than kiss him. His mind wandered over that delicious terrain without a single regret. With an effort he yanked his mind back on track and returned to his computer. Her current professional crisis needed his full attention.

On his desk, his phone chirped with another automatic update from the museum. Rush had set the program to send immediate alerts and all clears every six hours. The system was clear, no physical or technical glitches found. Their computer systems from administration to the electronic security measures remained virus-free.

"Behaviors," he muttered to himself. He downed another gulp of hot coffee. Without more data he couldn't get a full read on the hacker who had snooped State Department email and attempted to embarrass the US at the museum. Where else could he look?

He opened another search window on the computer and started over. They needed hard facts to go along with his gut instinct and Madison's professional insight. "Behaviors," he muttered. "Behaviors and anomalies."

"Is this a private conversation?"

Madison's voice at his back felt as warm as a ray of sunshine. Swiveling in the chair, he started to answer and went speechless at the sight. Her blond hair rumpled from sleep, she'd pulled on one of his faded black T-shirts, the hem riding high on her sexy thighs. She couldn't have anything on underneath it. His mouth watered and his body went hard.

"I didn't see a robe," she said, watching him closely.

"A perfect substitute," he managed. He wanted to turn her around and take her right back to the bedroom and never let her leave. She'd never want for anything. Neither would he.

"I'll, *um*, go change clothes and then you can catch me up."

The insecure side step toward the door brought him to his feet. He wrapped her in his arms and indulged the need, kissing her until she melted into him once more. "Nothing much to add yet," he admitted, drawing her hips snug against his.

She hummed and her eyes were soft and liquid when she looked up at him. "You might be my cure for coffee." She trailed a finger down the center of his chest. "Can I check the stitches?"

He let her lift his shirt and endured the gentle touches as she gave the healing wound a wide berth. "Well?"

"Looks good," she said.

"Told you." He tipped her chin up for another kiss, smoothed his hand down the soft column of her throat. Somehow he let her go without following her or telling her to hurry.

With the programs running, he killed the waiting time in the kitchen, searching for a breakfast solution. His usual day for grocery delivery was Monday and his supplies were low. She deserved better than the two best options of frozen pizza or cereal with a dash of milk.

She walked back into the kitchen, wearing a halter-top sundress in a blue as soft as the summer sky over the bay. Her hair was down and the golden waves framed her lovely face. His gaze skimmed down to find her feet were bare, that daisy taunting him again. He forced himself to assess the burn on her foot, pleased to see it was healing well.

Please, God, let her need help with this zipper tonight.

"You look like you're ready for a brunch date in the islands." Though he'd meant it as a compliment, she frowned at him, her eyebrows shading those glorious green eyes.

Was she having second thoughts about him? Last night? The next step? He forced his mind away from that gerbil wheel and focused on her. "Why don't we go for brunch?" he said, stopping awkwardly in front of her. "Let me change."

"We should stay in," she reminded him.

Right. "Then why are you dressed up?" She put his graphic tee and worn jeans to shame.

"Because I didn't really buy anything casual. It's either this or your tees." A blush stained her cheeks. "I need coffee," she said, scooting by him to reach the coffeepot.

He didn't see a zipper on this dress, probably because his mind was too busy conjuring the image of her wearing his T-shirt.

"Have your coffee," he said, surprised his voice didn't crack. He pulled his cell phone from his pocket and set it on the countertop. "Check the directory and make your choice for delivery."

She stared at the phone as if it might explode. "I can't get delivery in the middle of Sunday brunch rush. I'm not you."

"And the world rejoices." He grinned, came back and kissed her cheek. "Per the society page, you're my wife, remember? Whoever you call will deliver."

And if they didn't, he'd make sure they understood the gravity of the slight. He hustled to the bedroom before she could argue.

He chose khaki slacks and a white, short-sleeved polo shirt. He found his deck shoes in the closet and slid his watch over his wrist, his wallet into his pocket. They had a great deal of waiting ahead of them and the day was gorgeous. He decided they would take the Lamborghini for a drive along the coast after breakfast. Thankfully, Madison wasn't the type shallow enough to sell out as his wife for the wealth, but showing off a little and giving her a taste of how smooth life could be couldn't hurt his long game.

"That was fast," she said, her gaze cruising over him from head to toe when he returned to the kitchen.

"Fast isn't all bad," he said. "In the right context."

Her tongue darted over her lips and her cheeks colored again. He gave himself a point on the imaginary scoreboard in his head and picked up his phone. "How long do we have?"

Her gaze dropped to her coffee. "Maybe ten more minutes?"

"If I had my choice, we'd be going out." He leaned across the counter and smoothed a lock of her hair behind her ear. "We still can," he said.

She didn't lift her gaze. "I don't want you embarrassed if the FBI shows up. Or worse."

"You're innocent." He had to work to hide his frustration. "We'll prove it." He had to prove it sooner rather than later.

"I know." She backed away from his touch and hugged herself, effectively shutting him out.

Something snapped inside him and he re-ordered his day. He was letting his personal desire and pervasive loneliness shift the top priority. He couldn't waste time selfishly thinking of romantic drives when she so clearly needed a resolution.

"You stay here and eat." He opened the panel near the door and chose the keys to the Porsche. "I'll go in to the office and prove it."

She rounded the counter and hurried forward, catching his arm in her slender hands. "I'm not trying to insult you or ignore your generosity, Sam."

Generosity? That wasn't the word he'd use for last night. He swallowed the knee-jerk sarcastic response. "I know that." He toyed with the keys in his hand. Man up, he told himself. "You called me in to help you with the hacker." He'd blurred the lines, hoping to win her affection with a little time and superb sex. "Stay here. You'll be safe." Somehow he managed not to grab her close and kiss her goodbye.

"What happened to working together?" she asked.

"I'll focus better working alone." He used his phone to reset the security system for her.

Her curls swayed over her bare shoulders as she shook her head. "You need my input."

He shrugged. "I'll call when I hit that point."

He was walking out when the bell rang at the delivery door downstairs. He angled the camera and confirmed the restaurant logo on the ball cap and bag. He glanced down and saw Madison's feet were still bare. "I'll get it. Wait here."

Naturally, she didn't listen, slipping into the elevator with him. "I paid already and added a tip."

"You didn't put it on my account?"

"No." She shook her head. "Why would I do that?"

Because I'm your husband, he thought, unable to come up with a sane answer. For some reason, that made him angrier than her common sense about staying in for brunch. Irrational, but true. Silently, he cursed Spalding for being dumb enough to follow a hacker's trail and make Madison paranoid.

He heard her exclamation when the elevator doors parted on a standard building lobby. All glass and marble, staged with a desk, plants and a waiting area.

"Why go to the trouble when you live here alone?" she asked.

"In case I want to develop or sell," he answered. "Wait here." He tapped a code into the panel and opened the door to accept the delivery.

The deliveryman—woman, he noticed—smiled at him. "Good morning," she said politely.

"Hi," he replied. "They gave Nate a morning off?"

"Yes." The name tag on her shirt looked brand new, with Kellie printed in bright red on the white background. "Your wife's credit card did not go through."

"That's impossible."

In the reflection off the glass, Sam saw Madison rounding the corner. He waved her back. "Just put it on my account," he said.

"Yes, sir." The deliverywoman held out a small clipboard. "Sign here please."

"Sam!"

His hands occupied with clipboard and pen, Madison's warning saved him. He dodged when the deliverywoman swung the bag at his head and blocked with an elbow, trying to push her onto the street. He had to jump back when sunlight bounced off the blade of a knife in her hand. He was damn tired of knives.

"Hit the alarm," he shouted to Madison.

Kellie used the advantage, lunging into the lobby. He countered, using the clipboard to jab her and push her back to the door. He didn't want her to get away, yet he couldn't let her too close to Madison.

Kellie clearly had superb martial arts training, but Sam learned to fight dirty in juvie. As they circled, he judged the reach, the options. Get under the knife and he could do some damage. She was quicker than the mugger and had a clear, deadly intent about her.

She came at him in a flurry of limbs, slithering around him like mercury. The clipboard cracked in two when he used it to block a kick. Better than his jaw, he decided, tossing the pieces aside. Sam changed tactics, not playing to win, just buying time. All he had to do was keep Kellie busy and not die before help arrived. As she spun by him again, he landed a hard jab to her kidneys.

It only pissed her off. With a terror-inducing scream, she leaped at him, knife leading the way. He struck the elbow of her knife hand. Her grip held. Driving a fist into her gut, he heard her breath explode from her chest and still she snarled as she rolled to her feet.

He'd miscalculated his position and now she was between him and Madison. Why hadn't he shown Madison the safe room? He jerked, ready to chase down Kellie, but she didn't bolt for Madison. She remained fixed on him. He waited, determined to draw her to him like a bullfighter in the ring. He watched her coil and spring into another attack and fell back as the knife whizzed past his throat. He caught her ankle and yanked, dumping her on her face. She twisted and kicked out. He reached for that foot and missed. Her shoe scraped the side of his face and plowed into his shoulder.

He rolled with her, his only hope against the next arc of the knife, when he heard a muffled clang and her body went limp.

Sam looked up into Madison's furious face, letting his gaze trace down to the fire extinguisher she held in both hands. She was braced to deal another blow. "Is she out?"

"Kick that knife away." When Madison had the knife out of reach, Sam shook Kellie's limp leg, then extricated himself and stood up.

"Nice job," he said. "Thanks."

She blew a strand of hair from her face, unwilling to release her hold on her makeshift weapon. "You had her."

He wasn't so sure. "I let her too close to you." He pulled Madison into his arms. "I'm sorry. I should have shown you the safe room."

"I wouldn't have left you." She silenced his apologies and erased his regrets with a swift, hard kiss. "I'm fine, Sam. She was after *you*."

Chapter Eleven

While he processed her statement with a confused stare, Madison leaped into action, running her hands over his face, down his arms
and chest. She knew what she'd seen and that
woman had been after Sam. She was about to
reiterate that when a swarm of men poured
through the lobby doors. Uniformed police,
along with two men dressed in street clothes
and, to her dismay, Special Agent Spalding and
three men in FBI Windbreakers.

Two of the four from the San Francisco
Police Department cuffed the woman. They
bagged the knife as evidence and hauled her
away to an address specified by Spalding.

"Is there somewhere we can talk?" Spalding asked.

Madison ignored him, looking to Sam. "He should see a doctor before we do anything else."

Sam waved off her concern. "I'm good enough," he said. "Let's go upstairs."

She didn't want to spoil the serenity of Sam's condo by inviting Spalding and his team into the space. "Why don't we go to the office? After a trip to the doctor," she offered.

Spalding eyed them both, as if he wasn't sure where things stood. She wasn't about to put a definition on it for him.

"You can start here and now," Sam said. He slid his arm around her waist. "I'm not leaving until I know the lobby is secured."

Disgusted, Spalding shook his head, then turned and barked orders to the personnel working the scene. When Sam was satisfied, he led them around the corner to the elevators. Madison expected him to call the elevator they'd used to return to the condo, curious when he pressed the button for a different elevator. As they traveled up two floors according to the display above the door, Madison wondered how many secrets Sam had built into this building.

They exited the elevator into what appeared to be a standard office suite. She raised an eyebrow at the man playing her husband and almost missed the answering, fleeting smirk.

"How many cameras are on me right now?" Spalding asked, looking around.

Sam tipped his head as if counting. "You might be more concerned with the signal jammers."

"Seriously?" The FBI agent planted his hands on his hips.

"Take a seat," Madison said, leading by example. She settled into one of the four upholstered chairs surrounding a low table in a waiting area in front of the windows overlooking the front street. "How can I help you?" she said, determined to prove she had nothing to hide.

"You're married?" Spalding asked.

"You knew I was," she replied.

"Actually, nothing in our standard observation we ran before the reception confirmed it," he shot back.

Sam stood at her back. "Not even the marriage license on file in Nevada?"

"That has held up," Spalding allowed.

Madison felt like an insect about to get flattened as the FBI agent watched her. "What happened at my apartment?"

"Why do you maintain a separate residence from your husband?"

"Privacy," Sam answered before she could open her mouth. "In light of current events, you can see why we'd find it prudent."

Spalding cocked his head. "According to the neighbors, on the night of the reception a man was buzzed into the building. He pounded on your door, demanding you let him in."

"No one was buzzed in by Madison," Sam said. "We weren't there. Have you identified the man?"

Spalding shifted. "Yes. He was a low-level assistant at the Chinese consulate. His body was found this morning behind a garbage bin in an alley two blocks away."

"No." Madison's self-control fractured. Without Sam's palms on her shoulders she wouldn't know up from down. "Have you made some connection between that man and me?" She hated how her voice quavered.

"Not beyond his appearance at your door. What concerns me is the timing, Mrs. Goode."

"Bellemere," Sam corrected.

"We received a tip shortly after the reception ended that you've been taking bribes, Mrs. Bellemere," Spalding emphasized the last name with a glare for Sam. "Then this man comes to your door, apparently desperate and now he's dead."

"You know this wasn't her," Sam muttered.

The doubt was clear in Spalding's eyes. Madison swallowed around the panic in her throat. "You couldn't call and ask me about this directly?"

"You weren't there to ask," Spalding replied. "I'm asking now." He withdrew an envelope from his inner pocket. "Do you recognize any of these men?"

She studied each face, all of them with Asian features, none of them familiar. "No." She knew Spalding didn't believe her. "I'm excellent with faces," she said. "If these men were essential to the staff within the consulates I work with, I would know them. How can I help you close this investigation?"

"Our investigation is only getting started," Spalding evaded.

"You'll never be able to close the investigation if you keep chasing bogus tips," Sam snarled. "I'm calling our lawyer."

She appreciated his protective nature and the way he played his part as her husband with such dedication. "Did you receive the tip by email?"

Spalding tucked the pictures back into the envelope and the envelope back into his jacket. "Yes. We received another communication this morning that you were helping extricate a spy from the Chinese delegation."

"You believe the spy is the dead man?" She laughed. She clapped a hand over her mouth, but the hysterical giggles kept bubbling up. "Excuse me," she said, catching her breath. "First of all, you've interviewed my boss and coworkers by now. You must know an accusation like that is pure fiction. If it *were* true, it would be well above my pay grade."

"Your boss said the same thing."

She took comfort in his sincerity and pushed aside her fears to get a better read on him. "Can I be candid?" On her shoulders, Sam's hands tensed. Spalding seemed relieved by the offer, rolling a hand for her to continue. "My guess is you're investigating this absurd accusation for appearances only. You already know I'm innocent."

"We aren't finding anything to contradict that conclusion," Spalding allowed.

"If you drop it, the tipster will know we're onto him," she said.

"Yes." Spalding leaned back, holding up his

hands in surrender. "Candidly, the cyber team is having no luck with the hacker who targeted the exhibit. You didn't help us when you blocked him out with the added security," he said to Sam.

"My wife expressed a desire for the exhibit to be safe. I will always do what I can to support her."

Wife was an amazing word when Sam used it. It would take a valiant effort to remember their marriage was fake when they were alone again.

"Since the reception you've been attacked twice, am I right, Mr. Bellemere?"

Madison's intuition spiked with the new line of inquiry. Spalding knew more than he was willing to share.

"My bad luck for being in the news lately," Sam replied, blowing off two attempts on his life.

Spalding sat forward. "With your permission," he glanced up at Sam, "and with your assistance, I'd like to pull Mrs. Bellemere's banking records."

She caught herself before she looked around for a Mrs. Bellemere. "You want to bait a trap for the tipster or hacker or whatever group is behind this?"

"He agrees with me, sweetheart," Sam said, squeezing her shoulder. "The hacker—by any definition—is targeting you." Sam came around and sat down, obviously intrigued now. "There has to be a reason. We'll help."

Spalding's gaze narrowed. "Are you volunteering Gray Box resources or solely your individual efforts?"

Sam grinned. "You can't go wrong by either answer. Consider me a consultant to your cybercrime team. We can work out a payment schedule if you can't afford my standard fee up front."

"Sam," she murmured, shaking her head. "Don't do this. Not on the record. You've been attacked twice already since our marriage went public."

"Because I'm in the way and my well-known skills are a threat to the hacker's big plan." He reached out and took her hand. "Putting your bank records in jeopardy is far better than putting you personally in the line of fire."

She couldn't argue with his logic and yet it made her nervous. "What measures will you take to protect him?" she asked Special Agent Spalding.

"Us," Sam amended.

"I've had you both under surveillance since the initial tip came in," Spalding admitted.

"Pardon me?" She came to her feet and crowded Spalding. "Your team allowed Sam to be mugged and stabbed? That hardly encourages our trust. And today, you didn't even try to help. You didn't walk in until we knocked her out."

Spalding laced his fingers, tapped his thumbs together. "I know how it looks—"

She cut him off, gaining steam without raising her voice. "What about the real delivery person? Have you sent anyone to find out how that woman got a uniform and name tag? I want some ground rules. We'll need some assurances in writing or we'll handle this on our own."

Spalding jumped in when she paused for breath. "We're on the same team. I promise you we'll share everything we have," he said, aiming a look at Sam. "Unless you already know what we know?"

"He hasn't broken any of his promises," she snapped before Sam could say something to make Spalding wary. "I have one more question before we move forward."

"Yes?"

"Do you have a theory about why *I* have been the target of this scheme?"

"I believe the person, or persons, behind this feels as if they can abuse some perceived connection to you. It's something I'd like to review with you if you'll come to the office."

Her knees trembled a bit at the idea of voluntarily visiting the FBI office. She sat down, perched at the edge of her chair. "Do you believe Sam's intervention at the museum caused this person to escalate?" She was already creating a short list of people with the skill and reach necessary to pull off such a stunt. Unfortunately the list grew when she added in people with the resources to hire the talent.

"Someone is working very hard to make us believe you're abusing your position for personal gain."

It made no sense. The idea of someone maligning her was bad enough. Having confirmation that Sam's troubles were a direct result of her inviting him into the mess made her sick to her stomach. "Can we leave him out of it?" she asked.

"Not a chance." Sam caught her hand, held tight. "I have some ideas to corral this trouble-maker," he said, his fingers twitching as if the code was coming together in his mind already.

"Great. For convenience, we'll work at my office," Spalding said. "My team has traced the informant to IP addresses all over the world."

"You're not buying that, are you?" Sam asked. He flicked a hand. "I can sit right here and make people in England think I'm tucked up at the bar in their local pub. I'll go along and bring your team up to speed, but I'll work better in my own space."

"That's true," Madison said absently. She trusted Sam's safety to Gray Box security over the FBI at this rate. They'd come a long way from email viruses, haphazard attempts on firewalls to conflicting manifestos, fraud and murder in a short time frame.

"I'll keep you dialed in to my progress," he promised.

Before they could argue, Madison stepped in. "What can I do?" She wouldn't sit back and twiddle her thumbs while they did all the heavy lifting necessary to find the root of the problem.

Spalding sighed. "According to your boss,

you're one of the best at analysis and you have that personal X factor that makes you some paragon of diplomatic interaction. I believe the hacker knows you, is possibly afraid of you since your marriage went public. I need your expertise. While the tech geniuses can pin down the hacker's location, you and I can work the case from the personnel perspective."

Although she worried she was leading Sam into a legal trap, she knew they had to cooperate in any way possible.

"Mrs. Bellemere, I've been through your apartment, your office and your background." He paused, holding her gaze. "We need to show this hacker that I believe what he's spoon-feeding me so he makes a mistake."

She looked at Sam, hoping for confirmation or a dissenting opinion. He was scowling at his phone display.

"There is an event at the Vietnamese consulate tonight. I'd like you and your husband to join your boss and his wife for cocktails. I've cleared it with your boss."

She cringed, knowing Sam would hate that. "I can manage it alone," she said to Sam.

He turned the phone upside down on his thigh. "Not after this morning." He shook his head. "I don't care if Rush's top investigator and all his dark ops buddies are tailing you, we're not splitting up now."

She couldn't argue with him. Not while her heart did silly pirouettes in her chest over his declaration.

"With your permission, Mr. and Mrs. Belle-mere, I'd like to bring you both in," Spalding said. "Since the society page hit on Satur-day morning, there have been paparazzi and teams from the consulates hovering around your building. Our exit won't resemble an ar-rest," he added quickly. "Let's capitalize on the opportunity. Officially, we'll have a can-did conversation. Unofficially, Sam will meet with the cyber team while you and I sort out who's who in this drama."

"I need my purse and shoes," she said. "We'll meet you at the front doors in ten min-utes,"

"And you're stopping to pick up breakfast for us on the way," Sam added.

The FBI headquarters in San Francisco were modern and clean and although Special Agent Spalding had been grim in public, his friend-lier side returned as she and Sam wolfed down their breakfast at a table in the small conference room near his office. Although Sam gave her a quick kiss before moving off to confer with the cyber team, Madison felt the skepticism rolling off the FBI agent in charge as he watched them.

When she was alone with Spalding in his office, he rolled up a map of the city covering one wall to reveal a board with her official head shot surrounded by coworkers and associates from the foreign ministry divisions she served.

Panic flared and for a moment she was sure he'd fooled them. Sam had called Rush and had the legal team standing by, but it was little comfort right now. She braced for someone to cuff her and read her her rights. "That's intimidating."

"It's meant to be," Spalding admitted.

Madison was reluctantly impressed with what Spalding had accomplished in less than forty-eight hours. He had outlined all the key players at the consulates and their latest interactions with her. He also had left up the initial information from the anonymous tip.

"What are you thinking?"

She hesitated, even though she'd promised to cooperate. "These men followed us from the exhibit gala," she said, pointing to the Vietnamese team. "Does their consulate find me suspect, as well?"

"If you go by the round the clock surveillance, they are curious." Spalding removed his suit coat and draped it over his desk chair. He studied her, hands in his pockets. "They haven't admitted anything to me, of course. It would be helpful to know if they're having similar attacks on their systems."

She made a mental note to reach out directly when she got home.

"Not one person I've spoken with has anything untoward to say about you or your work," Spalding said. "Usually, I wouldn't consider that a good thing, but I've seen you in action. Your instincts at the museum were spot on. Either you were expecting the problem because you were in on it, or you've gained some expertise from your husband through the years."

"My knowledge is summed up by the fact that I know when to call in an expert." Turning back to the board, she thought of the stories—the good and the awkward—to go with nearly every face. "I've been liaison to these two consulates for nearly five years," she mused.

"From the interviews I'd say you've made real friendships."

"No." She shook her head. "Not friends, strong acquaintances. There tends to be frequent turnover with consular staff." She wished she was wearing one of her suits rather than this sundress for this meeting. "What's your end game?" she queried. At the startled lift of his eyebrows, she tapped the big board. "Everyone you've put on this board has diplomatic immunity, except me."

"The US has successfully prosecuted diplomats in the past."

She folded her arms over her chest. "We both know that is a rare occurrence. Someone out there is using me and making a mockery of foreign relationships. You started this board looking for a scapegoat."

His hesitation was all the confirmation she needed. "I started this board, Madison, because a solid tip told me you were a problem child. How long have you known Bellemere?"

"He tutored me in high school," she replied.

"In what subjects?"

That wary feeling returned tenfold. She faced him with the calm and composure her boss lauded. Her gut churned with nerves, but she'd be damned if Spalding knew it. "Math and computer science. Both subjects have changed quite a bit since I was a junior in high school."

"I'm aware." Spalding dragged out his chair and dropped into it. He pointed at the board. "You aren't going to throw anyone under the bus, are you?"

"No." She came over and took one of the chairs across from his desk. "I'm a professional, Special Agent Spalding. There are enough challenges with this situation already if you hope to make any charges stick. What do you have in mind?"

His candor startled her as he listed out the possibilities, all of them connected with fraud and criminal computer behavior. Making her banking vulnerable opened up a few international options, as well. "You're assuming this hacker is in the States," she said as the key to his case dawned on her.

"It's a long shot," Spalding admitted. "Although my team is on board with that theory." He leaned forward. "When do I get to hear your analysis?"

"My analysis hasn't changed much from the ornery stunt at the museum." She studied the board again. "The person orchestrating this is someone who knows the right buttons to push with the big-issue chatter but is interested in a more personal outcome. The people with the real access are either hiring a young person or unaware that someone young and cocky is using them."

She walked him through the personal relationships and business interests of the people he'd tacked on to that board. No one had any obvious reason to take such a convoluted route through her to stir up discord. "Even when the insults are subtle, the rhetoric is clear," she mused. "All of the countries with an interest in the rights and resources of the South China Sea know what's at stake. National pride and revenue top the list. Framing me doesn't fit with the usual up-front bluster or behind the scenes negotiating."

When Spalding's phone rang he ignored it and they continued to discuss the latest sound bites and agendas of the foreign delegates she knew. A few minutes later, Sam burst into the office and she had to assume the people trailing behind him belonged to Spalding's cyber team. "Answer your phone," he snapped at

Spalding. "He's in the States," he added. "I'll show you."

Sam took her hand and pulled her from the chair. "You're gonna love this." Clearly expecting the others to follow, he hurried out of the office. He was practically vibrating with excitement as he led her down the hall and into a stairwell. "You okay?" he asked in a whisper.

She nodded.

Sam pushed through a swinging door into a hallway with zero aesthetics beyond the glossy cream paint on the concrete block walls. He stopped short at the secure door at the end of the hall, waiting impatiently for Spalding to put a card to the panel and unlock the door.

The big square room had several stations similar to Sam's office at home and along one wall, monitors were set up for video conferencing. She had the feeling Sam's equipment and skill would still outdistance Spalding's team.

Sam reminded her of a kid bursting with pride over a perfect report card as he gave her a crash course on the program they were using to find the hacker. "He wants us to believe he's in the Philippines."

"My team found his code signature in use in Amsterdam."

"Both sites are bogus." Sam signaled another member of the cyber team. "Bring it up."

As the graphics filled the largest screen, Sam explained the origination of several attempts on the State Department software. "I don't believe any of these locations are legit. It gives us a starting point. I can work with this and pick up his trail."

"You did this in less than an hour?" Spalding squinted at the colors crisscrossing the world map.

"You have a great team," Sam said. "They pick up quick."

Madison clamped her lips together, smothering a giggle at his casual, unintentional arrogance.

"I don't see anything stateside."

Sam nodded to the man at the keyboard. "The sites used overseas are known cells for kids like this one. We can build on it," he repeated.

Madison caught Sam's eye. "Are we done?"

"No." Spalding answered, although she'd spoken to Sam. "Not until I have a suspect identified and under control. I'll be requesting your pay history this afternoon."

"I already did that," Sam said, oblivious of

Spalding's glare. "If he's in the State Department system, the hacker won't be able to resist pushing his luck for a look at your accounts. He'll want to tinker in there if only to give his tips more weight. We can use that for insight into tactics and motive." He checked his cell phone again and scowled. "I can use this. I need to get to my place. I've called my driver."

"Go work your magic," Spalding said. "Just be on time for cocktails tonight."

"We'll be there," Madison said.

Sam nearly hauled her out of the lab, then the building, his eyes on his phone the entire way. Hopefully she hadn't promised something she couldn't deliver. If she couldn't drag him away from his computers, she'd sneak out and handle the cocktail party on her own.

His attention didn't waver when the black sedan pulled up at the curb. As soon as they were in the car, she said to Jake, "To the condo, please."

"You got it, Mrs. B."

She wanted to laugh at the nickname the driver had given her, but instead she gave Sam's tough shoulder a shake. "What are you doing?"

"We have the programs running," he said.

"Museum and now the bank." He pushed his glasses to his forehead and rubbed his eyes. "It's not fast enough." He swore.

"Sam, what haven't you told me?"

He turned the phone and shuffled the information displayed, enlarging it until a spreadsheet filled the screen. He leaned close so she could see it too. "I can show you more when we get home, but I think this line is a countdown operation."

"To what?" she asked.

"Nothing good," he replied. "If I'm reading this right, the first deadline coincided with the reception and the second with the disturbance at your apartment."

An icy chill dripped down her spine and she shivered. "There's no reason to target me."

"That's what's happened." He looked up from the phone and met her gaze. "You're being set up. You, the office or the country. I can't be sure which, can't make a plan without more information."

"I'm scared," she admitted. For herself, her office and her country and for him.

He tossed the phone to the opposite seat and took her hand in his. "Me too."

"You are?" The raw honesty in his voice shocked her. "Scared of what?"

"Letting you down." He glanced at the boarded-up lobby door as they passed the front of his building. "I won't lie, this kid is good."

"You're better," she said with a quiet conviction. This wasn't the confidence of an infatuated girl coursing through her. It was the utter certainty of a woman who knew how amazing and lucky she was to have him on her side. She did all she could to let him see that radiating from her, to feel how much she believed in him.

"Maddie..." His brown eyes flashed with unspoken emotion.

The car bumped as Jake pulled into the garage and then they were around the corner, up the ramp and stopped at the elevator.

"All clear?" Sam asked.

"Yes, sir."

"That's your cue, genius." Madison kissed him lightly on the lips. "Let's get to work."

Whatever he'd been about to say, the moment had passed. She told herself she was relieved. She didn't want to know what he'd been about to say, wasn't sure she could cope with any more revelations or limitations just now.

For now, it was enough to love *him*. She knew she couldn't survive in a one-sided relationship long-term, but for now, she could manage. He liked her, that was obvious and they were great in bed, she thought with an inward smile. Loving him would make the show more convincing for anyone watching tonight, tomorrow or however long it took them to find the hacker.

Chapter Twelve

In his private computer lab, Sam worked through the afternoon. He'd called in reinforcements in the form of Rush and an extralarge sausage and black olive pizza. Together they'd isolated the countdown, though they weren't much closer to making an identification or finding the accurate location of the hacker.

After she'd gotten past the shock and awe of his lab, Madison had set herself up at another computer, creating a digital reconstruction of the investigation board in Spalding's office. Occasionally Sam heard her muttering or making notes; for the most part he blocked her out. Realizing that he could ignore her bothered him. On the one hand he was grateful that she wasn't distracting him and on the other hand he wondered what was wrong with him.

"Your building is all perfect and pretty again," Rush teased, pointing out an email with a picture of the completed repairs downstairs.

"Thanks for handling that," he said. "This guy isn't over twenty," he added, pushing his glasses up and rubbing at his tired eyes. "Well, I think the hacker is male. Either way, not over twenty. Can't be."

"I'll keep at it," Rush said. "You need to go upstairs and get dressed. Madison left half an hour ago."

"She did?" Sam swiveled around on the stool, more than a little unnerved he hadn't heard her leave.

"Go on and have fun."

"Fun." Cocktails with strangers while someone was playing a dangerous game didn't sound like fun. "Fun," he repeated as it dawned on him. He sat back down at the keyboard and typed in new parameters. "Behaviors. Fun. Follow these stops." He pulled up the map from the FBI. "He's been to these places."

"You got it."

"I have to tell her." Sam jumped back from the work counter and bolted for the stairs, ignoring Rush's laughter. "Madison will know what that means."

He stormed through the stair access door of the condo, calling her name. "Madison!" He turned for his office and bedroom to find her. "Madison?"

"Right here," she replied in that serene voice that smoothed over all his rough edges.

She was behind him, emerging from the guest room side of the condo. He did a double take, realizing he'd expected her to be in his room. Later, he told himself. They had a hacker to find. Then he saw the dress, the same dress as last night and his mind fixated on the idea of the lingerie she wore underneath. He cleared his throat. "Need any help with that zipper?"

She blushed. "Not yet." She tipped her head to put on her earring. The long spill of cool, sparkling silver caught his eye. "Lucy." She answered the question he hadn't yet asked. "The car will be here in fifteen minutes."

"I know. He's young," he blurted.

"You've thought so from the start."

Sam checked the wall clock and moved toward his bedroom. "Come on. I'll explain while I change clothes."

He stripped off his shirt on the way and had his jeans halfway down his hips when he caught her leaning in the doorway, her green eyes hot, her teeth buried in her lip. "Like the view?"

"Absolutely," she admitted in her unflappable way.

"You're in diplomat mode," he stated, stripping off his boxers and reaching to turn on the shower. In the mirror, he caught the sheer longing on her face when she thought he wasn't looking.

"I am." Her voice halted. "You were saying the hacker is young?"

He knew it wouldn't take much to get her out of the dress and into the shower with him, but that would wreck the schedule. He and Rush had discovered a countdown in place for this evening.

He turned the water to cold and cleaned up in record time. Toweling off, he walked her through the bouncing IP address locations and the creative code language and behaviors Sam had found unique to one person shadowing the hacker group. "I think he's been to the places he's using to bounce the signal."

"A globetrotting teenager."

"Isn't that common in your circles?" He pulled out a dark suit and dressed quickly, the task more challenging as his body responded so readily to the passion simmering in her gaze as she watched.

"Yes." Her eyebrows dipped and her lips pursed in thought. "Doesn't that give us a bigger pool of suspects?"

"Only if you know them all," he teased. "Rush and I used to be thrill-seeking teenagers, without the global access." He buttoned the dress shirt, tucked it into his slacks. "We put out a few things we hope will catch his attention." He found his cuff links. "Do I have to wear a tie?"

"Yes." She walked into his closet and pulled one from the organizer. Looping it over his head, she proceeded to tie it for him.

His mind spun out visions of making love to her right here, in the closet. Man, he had it bad. "That's a lot more enjoyable when you do it."

A sexy grin played at the corner of her lips. "Just wait until I take it off later."

He kissed her, long and deep, reveling in the way she kissed him back with those lush lips and her whole body pressed close. If he was lucky, all the words that kept jamming up in his head and throat would be clear to her in his actions. "Later it is," he agreed, resting his forehead against hers.

Consulate General of Vietnam, 8:40 p.m.

NORMALLY TWO MINUTES of cocktails and polite chatter would have Sam running for his noise-canceling headphones and a computer. Circulating and socializing with Madison on his arm was a completely different experience. Her warm and gracious manners put him at ease rather than on edge. The pride in her voice when she introduced him made him believe they'd married for love.

"You make this easy," he said quietly as she made another graceful exit from a conversation.

"Years of practice," she reminded him. "Do you need a break to check the phone?"

"No," he replied. It was true. "Rush knows what to do." He waited out another brief conversation. "You're pondering the hacker's ID, aren't you?"

"Among other things." She took a sip of her wine. "Spalding insisted we attend and I can't figure out why. No one seems troubled to see me. There hasn't been so much as an awkward pause in conversation. Even Mr. and Mrs. Liu are having a good time." She nodded to them across the room.

"Is anyone you expected to see missing?"

"No," she replied, smiling.

"Any party crashers?" he queried.

"Not one."

He could tell she was frustrated, though it didn't show at all on her face. "Well, maybe he wanted me to fully appreciate your skill with small talk." He marveled at her ability to make him feel included. He'd always been an outsider at these things. She introduced him to another couple, chatted and moved on again. "If Rush gets wind of this, you're likely to get a job offer," he said.

"Oh?" She paused in her scan of the room to peer up at him.

He winked. "Definitely. He'd give you a high-powered title along the lines of 'Certified Sam Handler.'" When she giggled he felt as if he'd slayed a dragon. "I wish there was dancing tonight."

Her lips parted. "You're kidding."

He angled his body closer, just enough to block her view of the room. "I'm not." Holding her hand, he ran his thumb over the wedding set. "I want to hold you, Madison. Forever."

"Sam, I can't. Not here."

I can't. The blatant plea in her eyes startled him. Silenced him. "Let's get some air," he suggested, unable to keep the stiffness out of his voice.

"Please."

On the terrace, with the breeze ruffling her golden hair, he resisted the temptation to try and voice his thoughts more eloquently. "When will we have done enough mingling to satisfy Spalding?" he asked with forced brightness.

"Fifteen minutes, maybe?"

She wouldn't meet his gaze and he knew it was because he'd pushed her. *Wrong place, wrong time*, he scolded himself. His phone hummed in his pocket and since they were alone on this corner of the terrace, he checked the display. "Rush is making progress." He showed her the current screenshot.

She snatched the phone from his hand, scrolling up and down the limited information on the display. "I know who it is."

"You do? Who?"

Inside the ballroom, the fire alarm sounded and the sprinklers came on. Guests in dripping finery ran for the terrace and exits as security teams scrambled. "The countdown," he muttered, shaking his head. "Brat."

"Now I'm positive." She tucked his phone back into his pocket and patted his chest. "Let's get you home so you can catch him."

Home. He'd wanted it to be her home too. *I can't.* The words cut deep. "Just a minute." He pulled out his phone and within seconds, the sprinklers were off, the alarm silenced. "There."

"Do I want to know how you did that?"

He shook his head.

"Oh, Sam." She reached up and touched his cheek, her eyes swimming with tears. "I love you," she whispered. She tugged on his tie, smiling as she brought his lips close enough to kiss.

Dumbfounded, he couldn't summon a response.

Her diplomatic mask fell back into place. With her hand at his elbow, she turned him to the growing crowd on the terrace. With her signature composure and his assistance, they calmed the guests and guided everyone inside to safety.

Whatever theory Spalding was testing by insisting she be here, Sam was sure she'd passed it with flying colors.

Chapter Thirteen

Monday, 3:15 p.m.

Madison hated the waiting. She trusted Sam with every detail of the plan, but sitting here in the depths of the Gray Box corporate headquarters with nothing to do was making her more nervous than necessary.

The hacker had taken the irresistible bait Sam and the FBI cyber team had trickled out. Everyone affected by the antics from the State Department to the consulates had quietly been brought up to speed in a face-to-face meeting with Spalding. Spokesmen from each consulate delivered precisely scripted responses that the media were circulating per the usual. Unless the hacker had a wire on Spalding, he had no idea they were onto him.

Still, the waiting for the location and enough proof to make an arrest was driving her batty. They'd been so busy since last night, carefully verifying the prime suspect's travels and correspondence without tipping him off, that they hadn't spoken at all about what she'd told Sam on the terrace. She'd said she *loved* him and he had stared at her, the proverbial deer caught in headlights.

Should she say it again? Try to explain how she could love him and yet not be able to stay with him?

"Take a seat," Sam said, startling her out of the internal debate.

He'd been demonstrating remarkable awareness of her since she wiggled that toe two nights ago and invited him to make love to her. Invited? Ha. Begged was more accurate, particularly last night. A nervous giggle bubbled out of her at the memories.

His desk chair squeaked a little as he swiveled around, stood up. "Come here."

She did, hoping he had worked kissing her senseless into the afternoon schedule. She needed the distraction. His hands light on her shoulders, he did kiss her. Quick and brisk, it wasn't nearly enough. "Sam."

He put a sleek tablet with Gray Box branding in her hands. "Start searching."

"For what?"

"An island getaway," he suggested with a shrug. "A place in the mountains would do."

Astonished, she stared at the phone. "Are you saying we need an escape hatch?"

He laughed, resuming his latest cat and mouse game with the hacker. "Only if you're wrong."

She groaned. What if she was wrong?

"You're not wrong," he reassured her as if he'd read her mind. "We've talked about it, verified his skill set, access and behavior. We can track all of the trouble right back to the day he visited your office with his father last year. You were convenient. Your system was a conduit he used and exploited. Every layer we peel back confirms your analysis, Madison. Jonathon Liu is the root of this mess."

"His father will be devastated," she murmured.

"Rightly so," Sam said. "There are consequences for interfering and tampering where you shouldn't be." He shot her a glance over his shoulder. "I know from experience, remember? I can promise you this kid is not a normal hacker. He incited people to violence and to do the legwork he couldn't. He needs to be stopped and then he needs help."

She knew he was right. "I won't snap," she said, coaching herself more than anything else.

"You exemplify fortitude," he said.

Her jaw dropped at the compliment. She didn't mind at all that he'd delivered it in that distracted manner he used when he was concentrating on something else. In fact, it somehow gave the compliment more credibility, as if it was as basic a truth as two plus two equaling four.

"Islands," he murmured. This time he wasn't talking about a getaway. "Damn. His creativity is off the charts." Sam's fingers flew over the keyboard.

She didn't hover, forcing herself to sit down with the tablet and do as he asked. Hawaii was lovely. At the moment, it wasn't far enough away.

When Spalding had Jonathon in custody, she wanted to go somewhere she'd never been. Somewhere isolated. She glanced at Sam, hoping he'd be willing to go with her. She studied each location, making sure the amenities he appreciated would be available. There were the Calendar Islands in Maine and summer was the best time to head out there. The Caribbean was never wrong and if he wanted seaside cliffs, there was always Ireland.

While he murmured at the screen, her attention was divided between the island debate and how to break the news to Mr. Liu that his son had turned into a criminal.

She heard the chime as the elevator arrived. Glancing up, she saw Rush striding over. "How is he doing?" he asked.

"He's in his element," she said. Holding up the tablet, she added, "He gave me a toy because I was hovering."

"She was pacing," Sam interjected without skipping a beat. "Hovering would've gotten her kicked out."

Rush grinned at her and then turned to Sam. "Have you found him yet?"

"Getting closer," Sam answered. "I know he's in town. I just have to prove it."

Rush caught her eye. "And if he's in the consulate?"

It was the biggest point of concern with their plan. If Mr. Liu's son was causing this trouble from somewhere inside the consulate, it would require a delicate negotiation to stop him. The consulate was technically outside US legal jurisdiction. "My boss has been assured China will respond swiftly even if we prove the culprit is in the consulate."

Rush moved closer to Sam's desk for a moment, then returned to her. "Officially, do you trust that assurance?"

"I have to." It wasn't ideal. She'd had a nightmare, dreading Mr. Liu's probable reaction to the news. "No system is perfect," she added softly.

Rush winked. "We've made sure Gray Box comes pretty damn close."

"If you were looking for an island, where would you go?" she asked, needing a lighter subject.

"Don't answer her," Sam said. "It's her choice."

"To buy or to visit?" Rush asked, ignoring him.

Madison looked up, saw he was serious and laughed. Rush and Sam were both so easygoing and down to earth that she occasionally forgot they were both billionaires. On the rare occasions when the super-wealthy mind-set appeared, it caught her off guard.

"To visit," she answered politely.

His gaze narrowed and he lowered his voice. "Are you looking to move out of the area?"

"No," she replied. There was a subtext here she was missing. "Sam mentioned a weekend getaway."

Sam snorted. "I've promised her a two-week excursion anywhere in the world."

"A weekend is definite. The rest depends on my boss approving the time off."

Rush's eyebrows lifted. "After your service record, you think there's any doubt?"

"Only in how and when things settle out with all of this." She swiped the tablet screen and tilted it to show him a picture, desperate to change the subject. "Trinidad and Tobago?"

"Never been there," Rush said. "I'll have to put it on my list."

"Got him!" Sam shouted.

Madison and Rush surged forward to flank him. "Seriously?"

"He's in Chinatown." Sam pulled over a laptop, ignoring them, while he continued working. "We just have to keep him there."

Rush held up a hand for a high five and Madison obliged, bouncing a little on her toes. It was almost over. Officially, she was thrilled. Personally, not so much. When Jonathon was in custody and things were sorted out, she'd indulge in that weekend with Sam and then the interlude was over. She'd return to her apartment and career and Sam would do the same.

"Anything I can do?" Rush asked.

"Extra eyes would be welcome at this point," Sam said. "I have it recorded for analysis later, but bring on the real-time assessment."

Madison distracted herself, watching them work. They were an excellent team, assessing and adjusting on the fly. Rush might be considered the face of the company and Sam the brain, but these recent days had proven to her they were equally committed and could manage either role well if necessary.

"Look," Rush said to Madison, pointing at a monitor coming to life with a grainy view outside an internet café. "Street cam. Live feed. You can watch the takedown."

"No view inside?" she asked, suddenly concerned.

"No."

Sam swore. "Hold. Hold. Hold." He keyed the same message into the FBI communication program.

"What's wrong?"

"He's one step better than I thought," Sam

groused. "Spring it," he said to Rush. He pulled off his headset and jumped out of the chair. "Come on, Mrs. Bellemere," he said, taking her hand. "We've got one more performance to give."

"What are you talking about?" she demanded when they were in the elevator.

He kissed her, hard and her body responded. Shamelessly, she leaned into him, her hands on his muscled shoulders. He wrapped his arms around her waist, keeping her close. "I didn't trust Liu. Jonathon," Sam clarified.

"Who would?"

"Right." The elevator chimed their arrival. "Follow my lead this time?"

"Of course." She nodded, utterly confused.

They stepped out onto the street-level lobby and Sam answered his phone with a rapid fire string of commands. Was he speaking with Rush or Spalding?

"We're almost out," he said furtively, heading for the front door. He was into the part, his grip on her hand so hard her bones ached in protest. They were in the airlock when Sam swore. "He's here."

He tugged her behind him. When he reached

for the door to get back inside, she heard the electronic locks slam into place.

"We're trapped?"

"No," Sam said.

Madison knew he was lying. Whatever he'd had in mind, this wasn't it.

An image of the South China Sea rippled into focus on the monitor installed to greet Gray Box visitors. "Yes, you are trapped, Mr. Bellemere." Although the voice was being distorted, she knew it was Jonathon. "And you thought you had all the answers. How fitting to beat you at your own game, right here in the house that hacking built."

"Drop it," Sam shouted, yanking on the doors. "You've lost. The FBI knows what you've done."

"Knowing it and proving it are not the same. I am untouchable. Your laws don't apply to me."

Sam's face had gone pale under the dark whiskers shading his jaw. "I'm sorry," he whispered at her ear. "Let her go," he shouted up at the camera positioned in the corner of the airlock.

Glass shattered with a shriek and she screamed. Sam swore, covering her with his bigger body. At the sting of splinters lancing her feet, she didn't want to think about what was happening to Sam. A loud boom brought down another panel in a sickening shower of glass.

Over Sam's shoulder, Madison saw Jonathon crossing the street, a device in one hand and a gun held at arm's length. Where was the backup, the FBI?

"I am untouchable." The monitors repeated the phrase over and over until she wanted to cover her ears.

She knew he intended to kill them. She knew he'd get away with it despite any number of witnesses or security cameras catching him in the act. With diplomatic immunity, he could do anything at all unless China disavowed him and handed him over to the US court system. For Mr. Liu's youngest son, she couldn't see that happening.

"Sam." He wouldn't even be here if she hadn't dragged him into the mess. Tears blurred her vision. "I'm sorry." She heard the gunshot at nearly the same time the lobby window behind her disintegrated.

The air exploded from her chest as Sam drove them through the broken window and into the scarce shelter of the wide open lobby.

He kept his body between her and the danger behind them. She'd never forgive herself if Sam died protecting her.

She heard shouted commands and pounding boots and the distorted voice on the monitor ceased at last.

"The cavalry arrives," Sam said, turning her face side to side. "Are you hurt?" he asked.

"No, not really." She shook her head. Her hands raced over him, came back bloody once more. "You are."

"Scratches," he promised. "I'm fine." He brushed her hair back from her face and kissed her tenderly. "You were so brave."

"This was staged?"

"Not this, exactly. Rush and I agreed to give him an irresistible target," Sam said. "I'm sorry, sweetheart. If we'd had any idea he'd turn violent, I would've left you downstairs."

Leaving him to clean up her mess alone. "I thought this was a together thing?"

He helped her to her feet and kissed her forehead. "It is."

"What will happen to Gray Box if it gets out the building itself was hacked?"

Sam grinned. "Rush and Lucy were handling those details."

His confidence soothed her. "His father will be heartbroken," she murmured, watching Spalding put handcuffs on Jonathon.

"We'll give him the proof and hope for the best," Sam said. "Let's get some of these scrapes and splinters treated before we give our statements."

Knowing he was right, knowing her time with him was nearly at an end, Madison wished Sam would say the words her heart craved. She knew it wasn't fair to expect so much so soon. Maybe if they took a weekend trip, they could talk about building a true relationship.

Or maybe she needed to accept the inevitable and allow Sam to return to the quiet, private life he preferred. Hopefully some time and space would make her path clear.

Chapter Fourteen

US Diplomatic Field Office, Wednesday, 7:30 p.m.

The butterflies in Madison's stomach were pushing the envelope of aerial maneuvers as she and Sam waited in a formal receiving room. Charles, her boss, had cornered her this morning, asking her and Sam to be available this evening. She didn't tell him she'd moved back to her apartment after a double-date dinner with Rush and Lucy Monday night. She failed to mention that she'd only exchanged text messages with Sam since Jonathon's arrest.

They had both needed the distance.

When Jake picked her up half an hour ago, Sam had been in the backseat, looking dashing as ever in a soft gray suit. He'd even chosen the tie he'd worn for cocktails. He'd held her hand, casually noted she still wore the wedding set and then reminded her she hadn't given him a weekend destination yet.

"Do you know what to expect?" he asked her now.

She shook her head. "Only that Mr. Liu wants a private word before returning to China." Without his son. His decision to allow the United States to prosecute still surprised her.

She couldn't imagine the disgrace Mr. Liu had to be feeling. Knowing him to be a proud man, she'd found his aloof nature a mask he'd used only on formal occasions. He'd always been kind and warm in their more casual interactions. It saddened her to know his son's misguided stunt would bring his career to an end. China had yet to name Mr. Liu's replacement and careful, thoughtful communication would be required to repair the relationship between the countries Jonathon had exploited.

She hoped the exhibit at the museum would not be withdrawn on principle.

"Relax."

Sam's whisper at her ear launched a fresh

flight of butterflies. She told them to wait their turn. This meeting would test her composure enough as it was.

The double doors opened and Mr. Liu entered, flanked by two men from his security detail. Her boss followed, flashing them an encouraging smile.

She wasn't surprised by the formal greeting and deep bow Mr. Liu offered, only that he honored her before Sam.

"I am thankful to both of you for my son's life," Mr. Liu began. "There is no excuse to be made on his behalf. Were he trustworthy, he would be here himself to apologize. In his absence, I extend my apologies to you, Mrs. Bellemere, Mr. Bellemere, for his unfortunate actions against you and your country."

Tears gleamed in the older man's eyes. Madison had to fight the urge to soothe him as a friend. Beside her, she sensed Sam was waging the same war.

"Mistakes of youth, with time and care, become the wisdom of men grown," Madison replied.

Mr. Liu's son had made a dreadful, misguided attempt to embarrass his father and stir up national ire against countries he perceived as enemies of a supreme nation. As Sam had said, such choices had consequences. All she could do now was trust those higher up and say a prayer that the Liu family recovered from their youngest son's blunder.

Mr. Liu turned to the man on his left, who placed a slim box in his hand. "In honor of your superb service and dedication as a liaison to our country, I offer this gift."

She opened the box and stared down at a white jade pendant carved with the Chinese character for *peace* nestled into the center of black silk. Surrounding the pendant was a bracelet of jade beads, alternating white and green and amber, smooth and luminous as pearls, with a centered space for the pendant. She held a treasure and they both knew it.

"I am deeply humbled and honored," she said to Mr. Liu. She wanted to toss formality out the window and give him a hug. Only training and his obvious grief stayed her. "You have given me a treasure beyond value, a lasting reminder of what trust and friendship are meant to be."

From his station near the door, her boss nodded his approval.

Without a word, Mr. Liu handed Sam a

smaller box. With another deep bow, he left the room with his men. When the doors closed, Madison relaxed and leaned into the immediate support Sam offered.

"You did great," he said.

The praise eased the sadness of her farewell to Mr. Liu. "What is it?"

Sam opened the box to find a jade tie pin. "Wow. What does this symbol mean?"

She smiled at him. "Prosperity."

"Safe bet. Hope no one's offended if I have it scanned for any electronic signatures before I wear it to the office."

She laughed and elbowed him. "Behave."

"Open yours again," he said. "That is stunning. Should it be in a museum?"

"Probably, but I'm not giving it up." She touched the edge of the silk lining the box. "This is my name followed by the characters for deep and abiding friendship."

"That covers it," he said, his palm warm at her back.

"You think so?"

"Definitely. It's how I've always seen you," he said.

She should be grateful to have that friendship from him. She was grateful. Having had more, she knew it wouldn't be enough. "I'll never see him again," she said, desperate to avoid her personal minefield.

She closed the box with a snap as her boss peeked into the room again. "You ready for round two?" he asked. "The group from Vietnam is in the elevator."

Sam set their gift boxes on the table under the window, near the floral arrangement. "We're set."

The meeting with the Vietnam diplomatic team was far more effusive and genial. They'd brought champagne and made a toast to long life and happiness for Sam and Madison and continued positive relations between their countries. Along with their thanks came more gifts.

Madison gasped at the long strand of pearls with a spacer for the jade pendant she'd received from Mr. Liu and a large, perfect pearl on a charm clasp that would complete the jade bracelet.

When they were done, Madison wanted to leap for joy. She kept her face in neutral when her boss walked back in. His relief clear, he extended his hand to each of them in turn. "My thanks to both of you," he said. "Sorry I don't have gifts. You two kept the peace in a volatile area. The world owes you, Madison. You too, Sam."

For the first time in her career, Madison didn't care about the good opinion of her boss, her country or the world at large. She was pleased and proud of Sam. He'd skillfully corralled a troubled young man on a violent bender. Weary of diplomacy, she was ready for a more personal and no less delicate, negotiation.

She'd put him on the spot naming him as her husband. His willingness to play along and stand by her until they figured it out had surprised her.

Even now, with his hand at the small of her back, she wondered how things would go once they left the office. The time away from him had been agony for her. She couldn't tell if he felt the same. Once they were alone, would he suggest they announce a quiet, quick divorce?

"Take a vacation, Madison," Charles said, snapping her attention back to the present. "I'm serious. You've earned it a dozen times over by now." He turned to Sam. "I don't want her back in the office before August."

"Why not?" Madison asked, aghast.

"It's paid leave," Charles said as if that explained it. "You'll need some time to rest up and rejuvenate before taking on your new responsibilities."

The news blindsided her. "I'm getting a promotion?"

"You don't want it?"

Happy excitement bubbled through her. "Yes! I didn't expect it."

"You earned it," he repeated.

This entire mess had been one risky stunt after another with more than their fair share of close calls thrown in. She hadn't been sure, until right now, that she'd have a job once the legalities were settled. Recovering swiftly, she smiled and said, "I'll want to see the terms."

Charles smiled broadly. "Of course. But if you pop in here before August, I'll have security haul you out with plenty of publicity on hand for the gossip rags."

"Got it. Forewarned and forearmed and all that." Sam took her hand. "I'll come up with something to keep her mind off work."

"You've both been invaluable," Charles said. "Take care of her for us, Sam."

SAM BREATHED A sigh of relief when they were done. He had to find a way to make his case that they should get married for real. He'd rehearsed the words with Rush and Lucy and still he couldn't seem to get them rolling.

His house didn't feel the same without her in it. He hadn't slept more than a few hours since she moved back to her apartment and his sleeplessness was affecting his work. But those weren't the right reasons. He wanted her to want him for *him*. He wanted that sweet "I love you" she'd given him to be real.

He understood how much she valued her career and he wanted her to have that. He understood why Madison had been honored so generously. He knew what others saw in her, though his reasons were rooted in his heart rather than public diplomatic interests. She was amazing as a liaison. If this situation had taught him anything, it was that they were an excellent team. That was something he'd never known could fit into his life.

She cared passionately about her role with the State Department. For her, the career was more than civic pride and the essential mission of keeping communication open as a path to peace. She never forgot the people involved in the complex equations and that set her apart.

"The gifts alone are a remarkable gesture of

cooperation," Sam said quietly. "You've made a significant, positive impact on each delegation."

"It's a chapter closed," she replied, turning to smile at him. "We wouldn't be here, with a happy ending all around, without your help."

The finality in her tone gave him pause. He wasn't ready to walk away or return to their previous status of exchanging annual Christmas e-cards. There had to be a way of encouraging her to come back to the condo. He suspected it would never feel like home again without her.

He hadn't handled the personal nuances well since she called him to the museum last week. He had to improve and quickly. Here, he had one more chance and he couldn't squander it. He'd promised to follow her lead and he'd done his best to honor that.

"Well," he said, gesturing to the car. "How should we celebrate?"

Chapter Fifteen

As Jake held open the car door, Madison slid across the seat to make room for Sam. "I'm overwhelmed," she admitted, pressing a hand to her belly. She wanted to celebrate with Sam, privately, for a long time.

"I need to be honest," Sam said. "Charles gave me a heads-up about the promotion and vacation. Rush has the plane and crew standing by and Lucy said she packed a suitcase for you to cover any locale or occasion." He reached to the opposite seat and handed her a leather portfolio. "Your passport, airport information, everything you need to go anywhere you like."

"And you?" she asked.

"I'll follow your lead."

The words sent a delicious tremor dancing over her skin. This was her moment, the private solitude she'd been hoping for to make her case for staying together.

"I even built you a clean laptop," he said, breaking the silence.

"You did?"

He dragged a finger over the back of her hand. "Absolutely. You need a fresh start."

Tears clogged her throat. She couldn't see any happiness in a fresh start without Sam, yet she couldn't seem to get the conversation started.

"Thanks for everything." She turned up her palm and wrapped her fingers around his hand. The scrapes from his fight with the delivery-woman were scabbed over, but she suspected his hands still ached. "You were amazing every step of the way. I don't even want to think about how awful things would be now without your help."

"I was just your technical backup. You and the FBI did the hard stuff."

"Now you're modest?"

He grinned, unrepentant. "We were a good team."

She shifted closer to him, leaning in to kiss his cheek. He brought her closer and caught her lips. She gave herself up to the heat and passion of him. If this was the last chance she had, she would take every inch he gave.

"What will you do with nearly three months off?" he asked, his fingers toying with the ends of her hair.

"That depends." Get married. Have a honeymoon. The thought burst into her mind along with an image of standing at the front of a church, exchanging rings with Sam. It was less elaborate and more real than her first visions of their wedding when she'd been seventeen. She had to be brave if she wanted her happy ending.

"Sam, when I figure out a destination, will you…will you come meet me?" Not quite how she'd practiced it in the mirror. The ring she'd worn for more than two years as a fake wife felt as heavy and awkward as a boulder on her finger. How was a real proposal supposed to go after pretending for so long?

He didn't reply, though she waited, her worry mounting.

Jake took the exit for the airport. She knew Sam would drop her off, let her go anywhere in the world. Giving him more time was the right solution, although the idea of another night without him made her stomach cramp.

Still, giving him space was the smarter play, she told herself as her heart pounded a denial in her chest. Being clingy wasn't a good answer. Just because she was ready to commit didn't mean he was. Being excellent lovers and sharing an affectionate bond might not be enough for him to build on.

Sam was different, private and she led a public life. Her work would always pull her from their time together. Worse, her work would pull him into the limelight—the one place he resisted above all. Loving him might not be enough to make up for that and she didn't want to lose him over careers. Decision made, she smothered her proposal. She'd put her shy, fake husband on the spot enough for one lifetime.

"We're here," he said as the car turned toward the hangars for private planes.

Too soon, she thought as he tipped up her chin and kissed her softly. The tenderness brought tears to her eyes as she felt the inevitable farewell in his touch.

The car rolled to a gentle stop and the kiss ended as Jake opened the door for them.

Sam didn't want to let her go, but they were here. Jake was loading her luggage into the plane. She'd invited him to join her. *Later.* He wasn't sure he could wait that long and yet he knew he'd wait forever. For her.

"Sam? Will you join me?"

He heard the reservation in her voice. She wasn't sure he'd like what she was about to say. Clenching his teeth against the inevitable, he forced himself to meet her gaze. "For a weekend?"

"Longer. If you like. I know you have projects to get back to."

Always diplomatic and thoughtful. "Sure. Just let me know where you end up."

Her hands clasped in front of her, the smile on her lips trembled. He would not beg her to stay with him; he loved her too much for that. All he had to do was man up, smile and give her whatever she asked for. He'd already removed their marriage record from the Nevada database.

"Thank you again, Sam, for everything."

The words landed like a punch to his sternum. "You're welcome."

"Sam—"

He held up a hand and stepped back. If she dragged this out, he'd lose his mind. Rush needed him to get the new software up and running so they could start planning the launch and marketing. He seized on the thought, trusting the technology to save him again. "Have a wonderful trip," he grumbled, stuffing his hands into his pockets.

"Sam." Her voice turned sharp. "Do you understand that I love you?"

Did he? She'd said the words, but he hadn't been sure if she meant she loved him as a friend and for what he'd done or if she *loved* him. Gazing into those lovely green eyes, he understood that friendship was a type of love. But was it a strong enough foundation to build on? Was friendship a powerful enough magnet to keep people together for a lifetime?

"I love you too," he said, blurting it out. *As my friend, as a lover, even as the fake wife who somehow made my real life brighter. I love you, Madison.* That was what he wanted her to know. He fisted his hands in his pockets. If he touched her, she'd know beyond all doubt how terrified he was of her rejection. "Where do you think you'll go?"

"That depends," she said again. Her teeth nipped at her lower lip, the way she used to do when she struggled over a new concept. She balanced on one foot. "Just one last question, Sam."

Man up, he told himself when he wanted to bolt. They were both alive and neither of them was headed to prison or exile. It was situation normal. They'd succeeded, she was a hero and he had a new product halfway developed.

She twisted the wedding set off her finger, tucking it into her jacket pocket. His heart shriveled in his chest. Apparently that phase of her life—*their lives*—was over.

"Sam Bellemere." Her voice cracked on his name. "Would you be my husband?" She swallowed. "Through politics or technology, as my friend and lover, in sunshine or computer labs, please share my life. I can't imagine any aspect of my world without you to come home to."

He stared into her serious green eyes, then down at her bare finger. Should he return the ring to her finger, the one she'd bought for herself? Did it matter? He'd buy her a wedding set for every day of the week if that was what she wanted.

"Say something," she prompted, her voice thick with tears.

"How about 'I do'?" He stepped up and fished the wedding set from her pocket. He slid the engagement solitaire back into place on her finger and pocketed the matching wedding band. "I researched engagement rings and wedding sets," he admitted. "Turns out I couldn't picture anything suiting you better than the one you've been wearing."

"You researched rings? For me?"

"Yes. It kept me entertained through the last couple of sleepless nights." He stroked his thumb over the back of her left hand. "It only confirmed what I knew. You have superb taste."

She kissed him, wrapping her arms around his neck. "Yes, I do." She brushed her nose to his. "Should I infer that your research meant you were going to propose?"

"It was on my mind," he admitted. "But I promised to follow your lead."

"True." She laid her hand gently over the healing wound on his side. "Although you bolted out in front more than once."

"That was teamwork," he said. He didn't want to argue or dwell on his faults, afraid she'd come to her senses about him. "I said yes," he reminded her, pulling her into another kiss before approaching the plane. "Now you're stuck with me, right here beside you." He stopped at the steps. "Where to?"

"Las Vegas," she said. "I don't want to waste

time and we should make things right with the records there."

"Already took care of that," he said, urging her up the stairs ahead of him. "I didn't want anything hanging over your head when we were finished. Although I doubt anyone would've been looking at that anymore."

"Our heads," she corrected. "We're a team. You've always been the only man for me."

He'd never heard sweeter words. With his hands on her slim hips, he guided her into the plush passenger area while the crew prepared for takeoff.

But they weren't alone. Rush and Lucy were waiting at the back of the cabin and Lucy was bouncing on her toes a bit. "She said yes?" she asked Sam.

Sam looked at Madison. "She asked me!"

Rush shook his hand, pulled him into a brotherly hug. "Have you called your mom?"

"Thought I'd send her a first class ticket by messenger in the morning."

"Great plan," Madison said. "Will the ticket and news arrive with flowers?"

"And her favorite chocolate truffles," Sam confirmed. "I promise she'll be half in love with you before she arrives." He moved to the sofa and drew Madison to sit beside him.

She laced her fingers through his. "I won't change my mind, love."

"I know." He brought her hand to his lips. "That doesn't make me less eager to make it officially official." She laughed, the sound music to his ears.

Rush popped open a bottle of champagne, Lucy passed out the filled flutes and the four of them shared a toast to love and happiness as the plane lifted into the evening sky.

* * * * *

Love Debra Webb & Regan Black?
Check out the bestselling
COLBY AGENCY *series:*

BRIDAL ARMOR
READY, AIM... I DO!
WOULD-BE CHRISTMAS WEDDING
GUNNING FOR THE GROOM
HEAVY ARTILLERY HUSBAND

Available now from Harlequin Intrigue!

Get 2 Free Books,
Plus 2 Free Gifts—
just for trying the Reader Service!

HP17R

Get 2 Free Books,

<u>Plus</u> 2 Free Gifts—

just for trying the Reader Service!

HARLEQUIN *Romance*

Get 2 Free Books,
Plus 2 Free Gifts—
just for trying the Reader Service!

HARLEQUIN *superromance*

HSRLP17

Get 2 Free Books,

WORLDWIDE LIBRARY®

Plus 2 Free Gifts—
just for trying the *Reader Service!*